Terror in Disguise 2

Pulled Back In

Terror in Disguise 2

Pulled Back In

By

Cherif Sidiali

www.hexagonblue.com

www.hexagonblue.com

This book

is dedicated to

all those risking everything

for justice and equality

Table of Contents

Chapter 1

THE PULL BACK

On April 17th, 2009 I found myself thrown in a car by two people on my way to work. They shoved me in the back seat of a black car parked on the opposite side of the street from my office. At the consulate, they took me to an office where as soon as I walked in, the first thing I saw was a file on the desk with my picture on it. The person leaning over the file said, "Mr. Karim, it's been awhile."

I did not respond.

"Have a seat," he offered.

He closed the file, stood up and said, "Do you know why you're here?"

I had a hunch why, but I didn't tell him.

"No, I don't." I said.

"Let me get straight to the point. Your work for us never ended, we gave you some time to cool things down after your first mission, but we always kept track of you," he continued.

"As far as I am concerned my job is done. The mission I was hired for was complete. That was the agreement, if I recall," I responded.

"No, it's not. So long as you agreed to work for us, the mission is never done until we say so." James Foster replied.

"Now, here is where you come in. We have information that someone by the name of Naim Darkaoui, a senior leader of an international terrorist organization known as "The Reformists", has been spotted in different countries including Afghanistan, Iraq, Russia and recently Kiev. His main job is buying weapons, including nuclear warheads, to resell them to other groups involved with terrorist operations. The last information we received two days ago told us he was in Kiev meeting with an arms dealer who goes by the name Aleks Demco. From the intelligence we received, this Reformist group is very active in many parts of the Arab region and is planning government takeovers in Afghanistan and Iraq. Now, this mission is especially difficult because these groups are going to create a major setback for the region and global stability, but also US interests will be at risk. This son of a b***ch has been planning this for some time from what we believe. We had him on the radar, but he knows how to play the system. He is not alone from what we know. He has connections all over the world."

"What's my role in all this? You have enough agents for this mission," Karim questioned.

"We need someone who is fluent in Arabic. Otherwise, our agents can be exposed. This guy Darkaoui is very smart; he will sense anything that's not normal. He was trained to smell when something is out of place and we don't want to take any chance with him to blow the mission," James replied.

"You were specifically referred by someone for this job. You will have all the necessary documents and supporting material for the mission. You will be in Kiev tomorrow. Everything is already arranged. The subject speaks Arabic and Russian but from what we know his Russian is not that good, so he always brings an interpreter with him to his meetings." James continued.

"You are Dani (Short for Madani) Hussein, born and raised in Jordan. You're an international arms dealer," James explained.

"You'll be introduced to him by our contact in Kiev. Her name is Polina Kolanko. She has been working for us for some time and knows exactly what to do. She has already been informed about your arrival. She speaks Arabic, French,

English and Armenian so you shouldn't have any communication problems," James continued.

"Once there, she'll take you to the safe house for a debrief and to get the plan in motion. The mission code is 'Bluebird'. There will be no direct contact or phone calls. We will arrange for communications whenever needed. In case of any problems, the safe house is where you will wait for further instructions. Understood?" James asked.

"Got it." Dani relented, knowing that ultimately, he could not say no.

"This is your new passport, ID and couple of credit cards," James said, handing Dani his new identity. "Good luck." he added.

Dani was dropped off in front of his building by the same agents. They didn't say anything to him. He got out of the car. The driver and his passenger were gone before he had a chance to set his foot on the curb. He walked to his apartment, sat down and pulled out his new documents. Staring at them brought back memories; the sadness and anger showed on his face. He sat there for a while before he threw them on the table and proceeded to gather a few of his belonging. The thought of fleeing tempted him for a minute, but James already made it clear they knew everything about him. They already found him; now he had to comply.

Chapter 2

THE JOURNEY

After almost five hours of flying. the next day he landed in Boryspil International Airport, about a half hour from the capital Kiev. At the airport, Polina was already checking her phone, comparing the picture that was uploaded to her phone with anyone who looked like Dani. It wasn't hard for her to spot him making his way out with the crowd. She took a moment before she approached him. Obviously, she wanted to make sure that Dani would also recognize her from a photo James showed him. They both exchanged a quick look as a sign of recognizing each other. Outside the airport, without a word exchanged, Polina waved down a cab, they hopped in it and headed towards Kiev. The hotel reservation was under Mr. Dani Hussein.

She handed him a secure phone and asked him not to use the hotel phone.

"Our meeting with the subject Darkaoui is set for this evening at 7 pm at Big Boy Club at the Rostok Palace of Culture, Harmatna," she said.

"This guy Darkaoui, apparently likes to party, so our contact set up the meeting at the Club," she continued.

"The contact's name is Dimitriov Boyko. He was hired by the Americans under a deal that saved his skin from a life sentence in jail for selling weapons and contract killings. I still don't trust him entirely," she explained.

Dani listened to her then said, "See you there at 7pm."

"The fewer the words, the better," he thought.

Polina added, "Our story is that we've known each other for 5 years – we've been buying arms from you."

The Laskavo Prosymo Inn was about five miles from the airport at the entrance of the city. Tucked in a corner of an alley that stretched with a shiny cobblestone walkway. With some fashion stores on each side of the street, the hotel had a unique charm of coziness and comfort. The lobby was spacious and inviting, decorated with big hand made pots in each corner with fresh multicolored flowers. Large frames with pictures of Kiev covered some of the walls displaying the city's history. The rooms were equally attractive. Although small, they were of a certain high taste in a place where one expected less.

Dani and Polina walked into the club at exactly 7 pm to find Dimitriov, Darkaoui and his interpreter sitting at the table in the corner. Dimitriov stood up, greeting the two while Darkaoui stayed seated. He was too proud and arrogant.

"This is Polina and Dani." Dimitriov initiated the introductions.

Darkaoui nodded his head as a sign of hello. His interpreter didn't speak. Polina and Dani sat down and immediately Dimitriov started the negotiations.

"What are you looking for?" Dani asked, looking at Darkaoui and not the interpreter so that he gets Darkaoui to speak. Although Dani spoke Arabic, he spoke to him in English, so Polina could understand what was going on because though she spoke formal Arabic, she did not know this Arabic dialect.

The interpreter jumped in, translating Dani's question.

"Close quarter battle receivers, 5.56x45mm, intercontinental ballistic missiles. Any quantity." Darkaoui quietly instructed his interpreter.

Dani took a quick glance at Polina and Dimitriov and said, "For the 5.56x45mm, it's not a problem, I can have those immediately, but for the ballistic I need more time. Those are difficult to come by," he continued.

Darkaoui looked at his interpreter and said, "You have seven days or no deal."

Dimitriov wanted to say something but was afraid Darkaoui would walk away.

Polina on the other hand, tried to convince Darkaoui that seven days was not enough time to find the missiles, but Darkaoui wasn't willing to budge. Dani agreed on one condition: half of the money should be paid immediately and the rest upon delivery. Darkaoui seemed to resist the idea but agreed.

"Here is the account information where the first half should be wired," Dani said, handing the interpreter the account information which had already been set up.

The transaction amount was $700 million dollars. Darkaoui did not seem to object to the number. He pulled his phone out of his pocket, dialed few numbers and briefly spoke in Arabic. He then turned to his interpreter and said, "The amount is acceptable."

The meeting lasted for about an hour. Both Polina and Dani left the club while Darkaoui, his interpreter and Dimitriov stayed behind.

"I'll be in touch," Dani said before leaving.

Darkaoui needed to know who Dani really was. Dimitriov knew Darkaoui didn't like to waste his time or be set up. He had known that about him soon after doing business with him. Darkaoui asked what Dimitriov knew about Dani and Polina as arms dealers.

"Polina bought weapons from him before and they have been doing business together for years. I know Polina. She would never do business with someone she didn't feel good about," Dimitriov said.

Darkaoui, although not entirely convinced, was at ease for the moment.

Without wasting any time, Polina took Dani to an old manufacturing building in the heart of town which belonged to an old, retired businessman. The building had been deserted for some time. The owner could not sell it or make it functional due to financial reasons. The US Secret Service, on the other hand, saw the building as a strategic place for its secret missions. The agency rented the building from the owner under the false assumption that it would be used as a lab for medical research. The building looked very business-like with a sign reading "Lab Corporation Unlimited." The offices and labs were fully equipped with workstations, medical devices and lab equipment. However, the long hallway that led to an underground space was known only to the agency; it was added after renting the space. To access the hidden area, a pad disguised as part of the wall was installed.

It could be activated from a remote control the size of a USB drive. Once the pad was activated, the front cover moved, exposing the screen for identification verification and security photos. Inside, Polina pulled up a chair, leaned forward to reach the bottom of the chair, and pressed a hidden switch which opened the bottom part of the chair. From there she grabbed a small laptop and typed in her 8-digit password to access the files.

"The documents contained surveillance pictures of Darkaoui meeting with Afghani rebels and Iraqi fighters. According to information provided by the intelligence, these were guerilla groups who had been on the agency watch list for some time," she said to Dani.

"We tried to record what they were talking about, but our contact suspected they were alerted that someone was on their track, so we never got the opportunity to record the conversation," she further explained.

"Who's this guy?" Dani questioned.

"Mosib Dole. Some call him 'The Axe' because of his martial arts training. He was born in the US and joined the agency about three years ago. He was sent to the Gulf region because he is familiar with that part of the world." Polina added.

"Can you zoom in on his left hand?" Dani asked.

"He can afford to wear a $20,000 Rolex watch." he commented. "He must do a good job for the agency. Who does Mosib report to?" Dani asked.

"Kate Fragrance," Polina responded. "She is one of the most senior people with the agency. I met her only once."

"Can you access his personal file? Bank accounts, relations and anything else you can find?" Dani wondered.

"It shouldn't be a problem," Polina replied.

Polina messaged her old friend working at the agency. Nancy Webster went through training with Polina and they had formed a lasting friendship.

"Hey, how is it going?" Polina asked.

After exchanging some jokes and laughter with Nancy, she said, "Listen, I need a favor. Can you find me any information you have about Mosib Dole? Banks accounts, connections, any relevant information?"

"Who is he?" Nancy asked.

"He worked the mission in the Gulf," Polina explained.

"Okay, let me see what I can find," Nancy replied, "Talk soon."

A day later Polina had some surprising information in front of her. Mosib had bank accounts in several countries, properties in major cities and his connections were all involved in illegal business operations.

"The scumbag," Polina said, fuming.

"Now that explains why the conversation of his meeting with the Afghan and Iraqi guerillas was never recorded," she continued.

"Mosib was not in the Gulf by coincidence," Dani said. "He set up that meeting for Darkaoui and had those pictures taken. Darkaoui and the guerilla groups knew about them."

"We need to let Kate know; this is treason." Polina suggested.

Dani assessed, "If you do, you'll blow the operation - especially Darkaoui' s plans, and we need him for now."

Polina agreed.

The time was now close to 10:45 pm when the two left the building. Dani headed to the hotel where he spent the night sifting through all the information. While on her way back, Polina called Dimitriov to find out what Darkaoui was up to.

"Any news?" she asked.

"No, but he wanted to know about your friend," said Dimitriov.

"Okay, keep an eye on him. I'll check back with you."
Polina hung up.

After two days in the hotel, Dani decided that renting
a place would be a much better way to avoid attracting any
unwanted attention. As a secret service agent, he was always
thinking that someone might be listening or watching. With
Polina's help, he rented a one-bedroom Dacha outside the
city. Although most Dachas usually come with running water
and electricity with an outside bathroom, this one was redone
to include a bathroom inside. The place was outside the city
on Osokorki, 90-Sadovaia 92, Kiev. From this location Dani
had easy access to the City Center and to 'Lab Corporation
Unlimited'.

Meanwhile, Darkaoui was still working to find out
who Dani was. He did not trust anyone, not even Dimitriov.
He contacted two of his people and put them to work. The
information Darkaoui received confirmed that Dani was an
international arms dealer.

A couple of days later, Dani decided it was time to
contact Darkaoui to get the contract under way.

"Hello?" Darkaoui answered.

"Dani here," he replied.

"Meet you in one hour. Head to the train station, get
off at the last stop, cross the street and walk to building 25. It

should take you 10 minutes. The code on the main entrance door is 315. Once you enter, take the left door, the code is 48. Press both numbers simultaneously. That is the only way to get in," Darkaoui instructed.

The building was the old-style architecture with sculpted wooden doors. Dani didn't have any problems finding it. Darkaoui did not bring his interpreter this time. They didn't shake hands and did not even say hello. Darkaoui got straight to the question.

"Are the weapons ready to be delivered?" Darkaoui asked.

"Did you wire the first half as agreed?" Dani questioned.

"When can you deliver?" Darkaoui countered.

"As soon as the first half is in the account." Dani reminded him.

Darkaoui once more pulled out his sophisticated phone, dialed a number and instructed, "Send the money." That is all he said.

A few minutes later, Dani pulled out his small secured phone to check if the wire was deposited to the account.

Darkaoui turned to Dani, "Delivery in seven days."

"I need at least 10 days to get the weapons here," Dani stated.

"No more than 10 days," Darkaoui replied

"I'll see what I can do." Dani responded.

"See you in 10 days," Darkaoui added before leaving the building, making sure that Dani understood.

Dani didn't respond.

"It's Dani" he said to Polina. "We're on for delivery in 10 days."

"Where?" she asked.

"I didn't tell him yet. I'll call him the day before." Dani replied.

Dani knew where the delivery would take place, but he wasn't ready to reveal the information. The shipment was to arrive in Kiev from a US military base, arranged by the US military and the CIA.

"Dobryy den," (good afternoon) the Ukrainian customs agent announced.

"Privet." (Hello) the driver replied, smiling.

"Dokumenty?" (documents) the customs agent asked.

The driver pulled the papers from the side door pocket and handed them to the agent from the window. The agent glanced at the papers quickly and handed them back keeping the envelope of cash that was stuck between the documents.

"Pereyekhat, Pereyekhat!" (move, move!) he waved to the driver without inspecting the truck. The cash he received was all that mattered to him.

The two people driving the truck pulled away from the border patrol when the driver contacted Dani saying, "the birds are free."

"Head toward the freight railway that connects Bulgaria and Hungary and wait for my call," Dani ordered.

"Got it," the driver said.

Halfway through the journey, Dani called the driver. "Change of plans," he said.

The trucks moved at a rather fast speed trying to make it on time as expected. Two hours later the driver pulled off the freeway onto a back road. The detour was part of the plan so the access to Hungary would be from the back side where it was easy not to be seen. But before the truck reached its destination, the driver and his companion were accosted by two unmarked cars with three people in each car carrying semi-automatic weapons. They blocked the road and ordered the truck driver out.

They moved quickly to the truck driven by the undercover CIA agent, they shot him in the head, killing him. The other person in the truck jumped out speaking to the armed men in Ukrainian, but he was shot too.

Dani's phone calls were never answered. He sensed that something was not right. He thought maybe Darkaoui knew the whereabouts of the weapons and intercepted them, or maybe something went wrong at the Ukrainian border. He even thought maybe Polina had something to do with it, but then again, he never told her where the weapons where or where they were going to be delivered. There was nothing he could do now except to wait, hoping he would soon get a call. Hours went by and there was no sign of the trucks. The time was now close to the delivery schedule; 11:45 pm was the time agreed on by Dani and Darkaoui. Dani decided to try a last phone call before he had to face Darkaoui.

"Hello!" A voice answered promptly.

"Who is this?" Dani asked.

"You want the weapons, the price is $1 billion," the voice said.

"Who the hell is this?" Dani asked, sounding angry.

"The shipment will be delivered to its destination once the money is ready," the voice added before hanging up.

Chapter 3

THE DISAPPEARANCE

Dani was now faced with a real problem. On one hand, Darkaoui already paid him half the money for the weapons and on the other hand, whoever called him had a substantial quantity of weapons that could end up in the wrong hands. He called Polina.

"Hey, the operation got screwed up, the weapons have been stolen," he reported.

"Stolen by whom?" She asked, surprised.

"No idea, but Darkaoui is expecting the delivery at 11:45 pm," he said.

Polina made a proposal. "Listen, I will meet Darkaoui and you figure out a plan. Where will he be?"

"The shipment was heading to the port," Dani replied.

"Where in the port?" She wanted more information.

"The back side. At 11:45 pm, turn your phone light on. Darkaoui knows that's the signal," Dani explained. "Try to hold him off until you hear from me," he added.

Polina showed up at the port as directed by Dani. She waited for a while but Darkaoui was nowhere to be seen. He never showed up to the meeting. Polina was concerned and she phoned Dani.

"He didn't show up," she said. "Did you call him?"

"He's not answering," Dani said.

"What's the plan?" she wondered.

"I am not sure, but something is up," Dani commented.

What Dani and Polina did not know was that Darkaoui received the same phone call Dani did. The caller told him that if he wanted the weapons, he would have to pay $700 million in cash.

Darkaoui was told the plan changed; his first thought went to Dani. He thought Dani decided to up the price for some reason. He didn't bother to find out at first and was not going to let that pass.

Two days later, Polina disappeared from her apartment. Darkaoui wanted Dani to know that he meant business.

"You must know by now that your friend is gone," Darkaoui announced.

"You want to see her again, get my weapons or my money back. You have 48 hours," he continued.

"If anything happens to her be certain that I will kill you wherever you are," Dani threatened.

"You have 48 hours," Darkaoui insisted.

Dani needed to come up with a plan quickly. Either the weapons or the money. He made his way to the safe house and called James.

As soon as James picked the phone, Dani said. "What happened to the weapons and the subject? The mission is screwed up," he continued.

The agency had someone else on the case that neither Dani nor Polina knew about. He kept James informed about everything that was going on.

"I am not sure what happened, everything was on schedule as planned. Someone is ahead of us. They kidnapped Polina," Dani reported.

"Who kidnapped her? "James asked.

"The subject," Dani replied. "He said in 48 hours if he doesn't get the weapons or the money, he'll kill her."

'Sh*t, if he kills her, we'll have a big problem on our hands," James said.

"She's the only one who was able to get close to him. We worked really hard to make that happen," James continued.

"Listen, there is a person by the name of Robbin Holmes," James explained. "He's not your typical agent. I wouldn't cross the line with him. You will find him at a restaurant called 'The Pelican.' He's there three times a week. His usual table is to the left of the main entrance. Just say 'Spain is beautiful'. He'll know who you are."

Right after the call with James, Dani made his way to the restaurant. He pushed the door open, entered the well-decorated, upscale restaurant. He was greeted by the Maître D.

"Good evening, sir," the Maître D said.

"Good evening," Dani replied.

"The reservation is under what name?" the Maître D questioned.

"Sorry, I don't have one," Dani apologetically replied.

"Let me see what I can do," the Maître D proposed.

He looked down at his note pad for a few seconds and looked back at Dani. "The only table I will have available will be ready in an hour."

Dani did not seem happy with that response.

He stuck his hand in his pocket and pulled out a $100 bill, setting it in front of the man.

"Oh, I forgot, we just had a cancellation few minutes ago. This way, sir," the Maître D led the way to the table.

"Enjoy your dinner sir," the Maître D said laying a fresh crisp linen napkin on Dani's lap.

"Thank you!" Dani replied with a smile.

The restaurant was full, but no sign of anyone who looked familiar to Dani. He ordered his dinner: house salad, fillet mignon with sautéed mushrooms and béarnaise sauce and a San Pellegrino. He didn't drink alcohol. While eating his salad, he glanced towards the door to see a medium build man in casual clothes walk in and sit down exactly where James said he would. He couldn't see his face, but Dani was quite sure it was him. He set his fork down and kept his eyes on the guy. A few seconds later he got up and started heading in the guy's direction. As he walked by, he dropped what seemed like a key. Picking it up he announced, "Spain is beautiful" and the guy turned and looked at Dani. They both froze as they came face to face.

Yes, it was Carl Hooper.

"Karim." Carl started the conversation.

"Dani, now, but I am sure you already know that," he said laughing. "What happened to you in Spain? I thought you were dead."

"No, they made it look that. The body was someone else."

"How long you've been in Kiev?" Dani asked.

"Three years now." Carl said. "So, the agency found you?" Carl joked with Dani.

"I didn't sign up for this. I was fine being out of all this mess." Dani said.

"Well, you know, once in you are really never out," Carl replied.

"So, I take it you know about the weapons deal? And now he has Polina." Dani continued. "We should have never brought those weapons through Ukraine."

"I knew something would happen. I told James that," Carl offered.

"So, you knew about the deal," Dani said.

"I was the one who had the idea of setting up the cover with Polina and Dimitriov as a connection to an international weapons dealer," Carl explained.

"Wait a minute, you brought me here? So, it was you who pulled me from Spain and put me on this mission?" Dani was more than a little upset.

"Sorry, I could not trust someone else with this mission. I had many reasons for telling James why you were the best person for this job. I could not let another agent jeopardize the mission," Carl explained to Dani.

Carl hadn't changed much. He looked the same; had gained a little weight and his hair was thinning on the top. He was still sharp in his thinking and very concise with details.

"Darkaoui is not an easy target." he told Dani. "He is a former secret agent with the Egyptian Secret Services who went rogue. He knows all the secret service tactics and uses them to his advantage. Not to mention that he was trained by the CIA in an agreement between the US government and the Egyptians."

"James didn't tell me that," Dani replied in surprise.

"The agency has a reputation to protect," Carl said. "Especially when an agent goes rogue," he continued.

Carl and Dani were now up against someone who could be a real threat to their new mission of finding Polina and the missing weapons. Holding Polina gave Darkaoui a greater advantage in calling the shots. Both Carl and Dani needed to move fast to figure out what Darkaoui's plan was. Dani suggested that they should find him and eliminate him, but Carl suggested a different strategy. He wanted to get to the people Darkaoui was supplying with weapons. Darkaoui could have been eliminated a long time ago by the agency, he explained to Dani, but we need to know who's behind the scenes.

They headed back to the safe building with the idea that looking once again at the files might lead them to some information or a hint they missed. They spent some time looking at the pictures of Darkaoui and others on the computer screen, going over and over the classified information provided by the agency, but nothing clicked, until Carl said, "Wait a minute, what about this Dimitriov Boyko?" Carl asked.

Carl immediately pulled Dimitriov's information. "What do you know about this guy?" he asked.

"Polina told me he agreed to work with the agency as an insider after cutting a deal that got him off a life sentence for contract killings and arms smuggling."

"Can you get a hold of Darkaoui?" Carl asked. "Tell him you found the weapons, but you need few days to get them back."

Early next morning, Dani phoned Darkaoui. Several rings and no response. He waited a few minutes and called again.

"Hello?" Darkaoui answered.

"Dani here. I found the weapons, but I need three to four days to get them back. Where is Polina?" he asked.

"No more than two days or you know what happens to your friend," Darkaoui said.

"Let me talk to her," Dani insisted.

"You have two days," Darkaoui replied, ending the call.

Meanwhile Dimitriov was nowhere to be found. He disappeared after that meeting with Polina, Dani and Darkaoui. He knew that it was a matter of time before he was classified as wanted. So, he bought a plane ticket to Russia which he never used. He purposely used his credit card so his purchase could be traced, but he never left Kiev. He knew where to hide. His girlfriend Sacha had a cabin outside of town that she rarely used. It was passed on to her by her parents. Dimitriov and Sacha went there a few times when they needed to get away. He was not sure what to do but for the moment he felt no one would get to him there. His apartment had been turned upside down; not by the agents but by whoever was trying to find Dimitriov before the agency did. His desk drawers were empty and left open. He probably took everything from those drawers before fleeing. Even the $140,000 dollars in his account was all drawn out and the account closed.

Now Carl and Dani were convinced that Dimitriov had something to do with the weapons for two reasons. One, whoever was in his apartment is looking for the same thing and two, he fled the country; they believed, from the ticket purchase information. The problem for Carl and Dani was now how to get to him in Russia -and where in Russia?

Dani was up for heading to Russia, but Carl once again needed some time to figure things out. He needed to exhaust all his options in Kiev before hopping on a plane to Russia. Working with the KGB wasn't his top priority as he had worked with them before and had never agreed with anything they did.

"We need to find everything there is to know about this son of a b**ch, Carl told Dani.

"Who he knows, places he goes to, who he talks to, anything," Carl continued.

The first place they went was back to the apartment. Carl wanted to visit the place one more time. They checked every corner of every room, even under the sink bathroom, but found nothing. They stood in the living room to consider if there was anything they could have missed that would lead them to Dimitriov. Carl walked back and forth between the living room and the tiny kitchen but kept silent as if he was drawing a map of the place in his mind. With his eyes fixed on the shiny glass coffee table sitting in front of him, he noticed a slight difference in the uneven positioning of the two back legs of the table. He didn't give it much attention at first, but his trained spy eyes and his attention to the smallest detail made him curious why that table was uneven, even though it was almost unnoticeable to anyone else in the room. He walked toward the table trying to adjust it, moved it around couple of times, then decided to look closer, when he stepped on what seemed to be a bumpy spot. He stepped on it again hearing a crunching and popping noise under the rug covering the titled floor. He called Dani to help him lift the table, removed the rug to find a square of four tiles sitting loosely unsecured to the ground. Carl pulled the first one, revealing a stash of cash and a gun. He removed the remaining tiles and pulled out a black leather computer bag. He opened it and removed a small laptop from the inside and what appeared to be a phone agenda. Access to any files contained in the laptop were secured with a password so there was no way for Carl or Dany to find out what was in those files immediately. The phone agenda had some Ukrainian names and other South Asian sounding names. There were also some notes written in Ukrainian. Carl and Dani put the computer, the phone agenda, the cash and the gun in the bag and headed out, hurrying to break into the computer to find out what information it contained.

"We need to contact someone from the agency to unlock this computer," Carl said.

"I can get someone without going through the agency," Dani suggested.

Dani suspected that someone at the agency may be a threat to the operation if the computer files were accessed and Carl agreed.

Chapter 4

THE DOCUMENTS

Dani contacted his friend in Spain. Morino Caballero, who had two passions: music and technology. Morino was a well-known hacker who on many occasions was asked by the Spanish government to help with high profile national security cases or in bringing down mob operations. He met Dani in one of the operations coordinated between the US and the Spanish governments, unfolding a terror plot in the Spanish capital, Madrid. They connected the first time they met and had kept a close friendship since.

Morino did not hesitate to get involved as soon as Dani asked. The challenge, however, was that the case had nothing to do with the Spanish government, and all information was classified. But Carl had to find a way to unlock that computer and had no time to go through the protocol or play the waiting game for the agency to find someone. He hired Morino for the job. The following day, Morino arrived in Kiev. He had never been there. The interesting thing, however, is that he spoke Ukrainian, which he learned dating a Ukrainian exchange student in Spain for two years. Most people who speak the Ukrainian language also speak and understand the Russian language and that's how Morino learned Russian also. As soon as Morino showed up Carl and Dani put him to work. Carl decided that setting up shop in a hotel room was better than going to the safe house for security. After few hours, Morino was able to access the locked laptop. The files revealed key information that Carl and Dani believed would help them in their mission. Included were names of people involved, foreign bank accounts, and printed emails containing communication between key Russians and Ukrainian weapon dealers. Both Dimitriov and Darkaoui's names were on those emails.

The emails also listed another person with the name Griffin Garson, a US citizen and a drug lord jailed in Ukraine for leading a notorious drug and murder gang. His fluency in the Ukrainian language gave him an advantage with the Ukrainian mob. Griffin's time in jail was not a punishment, but an opportunity for him to build new relations with high-profile Ukrainian criminals dealing in all kinds of illegal activities. Once out of jail, he had continued conducting his illegal operations which made him quite wealthy. One day he received a call for a job to supply fake US passports for some people to enter the US. In exchange Griffin would be paid for his work in cash. Whoever hired him knew that Griffin could deliver. Griffin demanded $20,000 for each fake passport, half up front and the other half on delivery. The interested person did not argue with Griffin's amount or conditions. Griffin had the skills for the job. All he needed was photos for the passports, names and other information. Through his Ukrainian connections in the counterfeit market, he already had an expert in this kind of work.

Griffin met with Oleg Volkov one evening to discuss the details of the deals. They met at Griffin's place. Oleg arrived at 8 pm.

"Hey, Griffin," Oleg greeted him in Ukrainian. Oleg walked in and Griffin took a quick look left and right outside before closing the door.

The conversation was casual, starting with some questions and answers regarding each one of their recent life events. A few minutes later Oleg wanted to find out what was on Griffin's mind.

"You said you needed some papers?" Oleg pressed. "What are we talking about?" he continued.

"This is no ordinary order," Griffin explained. "I have people interested in passports," he said.

"What kind of passports?" Oleg asked.

"US passports. Can you deliver?" Griffin questioned.

Everything has a price. Oleg wanted to make sure that this was not a favor. He took few steps back and forth thinking for few seconds and requested $10,000 per passport.

Griffin hesitated. "That's way more than what they want to pay. They won't go for it."

Oleg was not going to negotiate on his position. "Talk to these people and get back to me," he offered.

"You're making more than what I am getting from the deal," Griffin lied to Oleg.

"This is a risky operation, as you know," Oleg replied. As soon as Oleg stepped out, Griffin dial his buyer's number.

"The people providing the documents asked for $30,000 per person." Griffin continued, "I don't think that's doable."

The buyer replied, "I'll have to check. When can they deliver?"

"As soon as they get half the money down, they can schedule the delivery," Griffin confirmed.

Griffin did not want any bank deposit; all his deals were in cash. He asked that the money would be delivered in cash so no trace would be left. A couple of days after the conversation, Griffin received a phone call saying that the deal was on. The purpose of the call was also to arrange a time and a place where the two could meet. They agreed to meet at an abandoned ferry dock just outside of town.

This was the first time they met in person. Dimitriov got Griffin's contact through a Ukrainian connection who had been jailed with Griffin. The Ukrainian gangster was Dimitriov's cousin. He and Griffin built a good relationship as they conducted illegal operations inside the jail with the help of two guards who were handsomely compensated for looking the other way. One day Dimitriov came to see his cousin in jail to address some unfinished business. Whenever Dimitriov needed something illegal done outside he would pay a visit to his cousin. They never talked by phone for fear that the conversation would be recorded. He would go and see him in person. And that's how he came across Griffin. Dimitriov's cousin knew when Griffin was going to be released and gave Griffin's contact info to Dimitriov. The cousin's expectation, however, was that he would get his cut from any deal Dimitriov will do with Griffin. This was an expectation that never materialized for the cousin because he died few weeks later in jail from reportedly an unknown cause, but the word got around that he was poisoned. Dimitriov was a person with no remorse. He would eliminate his own family member for a buck. It turned out that his cousin double crossed him on some deal with other

Ukrainians which Dimitriov learned about from a source who knew the whole story. Well, Dimitriov's visit to his cousin was not one of courtesy but to confront him for the last time. He brought him a carton of cigarettes, some of which were poisoned. The guards checked the carton, but they were not able to detect that some of those cigarettes were injected with Ricin.

A couple of days later, Griffin received a call from Dimitriov giving him the green light to proceed with the operation. He immediately contacted Oleg.

"We're good to go," he said.

"Where's my half down?" Oleg demanded.

"Let's meet tomorrow at the usual place, "Griffin offered.

Griffin had already told Dimitriov that nothing would happen without the first installment being paid and Dimitriov agreed. They met that same evening on the outskirts of town in parking lot where Dimitriov handed the cash to Griffin. Griffin was not a very trusting person. He sat in his car and started counting the money while Dimitriov keeping a wide-open eye on him. He lit up a cigarette and stood there silently.

Once the money was accounted for, Dimitriov asked "when do I get my stuff?"

"Give me three days," Griffin replied.

"I will expect your call in three days," Dimitriov said in a threatening tone, letting Griffin know that he meant only three days.

Each went their own way. Dimitriov contacted Darkaoui to update him about the deal. The next day, as planned, Oleg showed up at Griffin's to collect his down payment. He arrived at Griffin's apartment late in the evening, rang the bell and waited for few minutes before Griffin opened the door, totally drunk.

"Come in," he offered Oleg.

Oleg walked in and stood by the dining room table.

"I have to run", he replied. "I need to take care of something" making up an excuse. "You have the money?" Oleg asked.

Griffin reached in the dining room table drawer pulling out an envelope with the amount and handed it to Oleg. He counted it and stuck it in his pocket.

"I need the papers in three days," Griffin said.

"Three days is not enough," Oleg replied.

"No, no, these people are expecting the papers in three days. I have to deliver them in three days," Griffin insisted.

Heaving a big sigh, Oleg said "wait a second." He pulled out his phone and dialed a number. Speaking in

Ukrainian, he asked, "can you have the stuff ready in three days?" Whoever he was talking to said, "it will cost extra."

Oleg, turned to Griffin and said, "if you want the papers in three days, it will cost extra."

At that point, Griffin started cursing and yelling, then said "how much extra?" knowing that he had no choice except to pay since Dimitriov gave him three days.

Oleg back on the phone asked, "how much?"

"$3,000" the person on the phone said.

Oleg announced the amount to Griffin. Griffin, continuing to curse, agreed to the amount. "Just get me the s**t in 3 days."

Oleg gave the green light to the person on the phone to go ahead.

The new twist in the cost did not sit well with Griffin and he wanted to get that extra money form Dimitriov. He contacted him, but Dimitriov didn't want to even listen.

Yelling at Griffin, he said, "that's your problem, we agreed on the amount and that's it."

For the first time Griffin seemed to have lost money in a deal, but he wasn't about to let it go. He had to get his money from someone by any means he could. He decided to wait. Three days later Oleg brought the fake documents as planned, both Oleg and Griffin sat down, went through the documents, everything looked legit. Name, passport numbers and pictures looked very authentic. The condition, however, for these documents to be used, was that the people with these passports must come through Mexico instead of flying directly to the US. The Mexican border seemed less strict. Oleg handed the papers to Griffin and demanded the rest of the money; however, Griffin didn't have the remaining amount available until next day. Oleg didn't like that very much and demanded to keep the papers until the next day. Griffin tried to convince him otherwise, but Oleg refused. On his way out, Griffin walked behind him, covered Oleg's mouth with his hand and stabbed him in the back with a pair of scissors. Oleg stumbled to the ground, falling on his knees with blood running everywhere. He died a few seconds later. Griffin dragged Oleg's body to his car and threw him in the trunk. He then returned to clean up the blood, shoved the fake documents in his jacket pocket. Rushing to his car, he called Dimitriov

"I have your stuff. Let's meet at the same place. Bring the rest of the money," he said.

He drove at a high speed almost losing control of his car after taking a turn. After about 25 minutes he pulled into the meeting spot. His hands were shaking. He waited a few minutes before Dimitriov pulled up. Griffin grabbed the documents from his pocket and exchanged them for the rest of the money. Dimitriov checked the papers and seemed satisfied with the result.

"Oh, one more thing, your people need to come through Mexico instead of flying directly to the US."

"Why Mexico?" Dimitriov asked.

"For some reason, the Mexican border is easier to get through."

Dimitriov left while Griffin waited there. He needed to get rid of the body in his trunk. Once again, he dragged it to the pier and threw it over the guardrail. He was now satisfied that he got back more than the $3,000 extra he paid for the three-day delivery. Dimitriov, on the other hand, called the person who ordered the passports

"When can we meet?" he asked.

"He'll have your money," he added before Dimitriov asked.

Less than 24 hours later Dimitriov received a phone call. "Hello?" He answered.

"Bring the papers to the Podolski Hostel. You know where it is?"

"Yes," Dimitriov replied.

"Room 319, two knocks, and make sure you're not followed," the stranger ordered.

That same evening after the phone call Dimitriov walked in to the Podolski.

He was greeted by the doorman. He made his way to the 3rd floor. As ordered, he knocked twice when a young guy opened the door. He didn't say much. "You have the papers?" was the only question.

"You have the money?" Dimitriov asked.

The young guy threw a pile of cash on the bed and extended his hand to get the documents. As Dimitriov stuck his hand in his coat pocket to pull out the documents, the young guy was fast enough to pull out his gun in case Dimitriov was up to no good.

Dimitriov smiled, saying, "relax," pulling out the papers and slowly handing them to the guy. He took a quick glance at them while keeping a close watch on Dimitriov. He told Dimitriov to take his cash and leave, but Dimitriov was not going to move before he made sure his money was all accounted for. He counted it and walked out.

Dani and Carl currently were both trying to locate the weapons. The only way to do that was to find Dimitriov. Days went by with Carl and Dani trying to figure out a plan to get to him. However, the mistake Dimitriov made that he never suspected would come back and haunt him - was that he didn't think that Griffin knew his whereabouts. A well-connected mob leader, his connections could get any information he wanted.

The list Carl and Dani found in Dimitriov's apartment was a start to hunting down Dimitriov. They went through the entire list, but no name attracted their attention as much as Griffin Garson. On an early morning, a US secret agent stormed Griffin's place in Kiev, arresting him while he was still in bed. Although, they didn't have a valid motive for his arrest, they made one up. Their motive was that they suspected he was connected to an international terrorist group planning to attack US interests in Ukraine.

They started by asking him about his relationship to Adamchuk Boyko, a mob leader specializing in international arms trafficking, but soon they brought up the name of Dimitriov Boyko. At first, he denied any relationship to Dimitriov but as soon as they mentioned that they found his name on a list Dimitriov had, he panicked.

"Yes, I knew him from some work I did for him in the past," he said.

"What work was that?" Dani asked.

"He needed some papers", Griffin replied.

"What kind of papers?" Carl asked.

"Passports," Griffin said in frustration.

"Who are these people?" Dani pressed.

"I don't know; some foreign names," Griffin replied.

"Does the name Darkaoui or Mois Dole mean anything to you?" Dani asked?

"No, never heard of them." Griffin said.

"Where do we find Dimitriov?" Dani asked.

"I don't know, I haven't seen or talked to him for a long time," Griffin lied.

"Don't play smart with us", Dani said, raising his voice.

Chapter 5

THE BLACKMAIL

"You know we can put you back in the same cell in jail you spent time in. We have no problems getting you back there tonight if you don't tell us what we need to know," said Dani, blackmailing Griffin.

Griffin kept silent for a moment, then said, "The last thing I heard about him is that he bought a flat in Pripyat. This was all Carl and Dani needed to know to start their hunt. While still holding Griffin, Dani told Carl he was going to Pripyat that same night. He enlisted two more agents and the three headed straight to Pripyat.

Almost three hours later they arrived at the abandoned town. They sat in the car waiting to see if anyone resembling Dimitriov showed up. It was an all-night stake out. The next morning as Dani got out of the car to stretch, he noticed someone wearing a long coat and a baseball cap. At first, he didn't think twice about that person, but decided to check him out. He followed him closely. As soon the stranger noticed someone following him, he picked up the pace. After a few blocks of this foot race, Dimitriov was pinned against the wall by the other two CIA agents who saw Dani chasing him. He tried to fight his way out but was subdued by the three of them. They handcuffed him and put him in the back between the two CIA agents. Now with Dimitriov in custody, Carl and Dani finally could get some answers.

"What am I charged with?" Dimitriov wanted to know.

"Where should we start?" Carl asked. "The illegal drugs, the weapons, maybe the fake documents hidden in your apartment, your connection to Griffin Garson, or would you rather tell us everything?"

"I don't know any of these people you mentioned," Dimitriov argued.

"Listen, you better come clean," Dani suggested. "We know everything about you, so your game of denying it doesn't stand a chance," he continued.

Dimitriov in a low voice, start swearing in Ukrainian.

"How do you know Griffin?" Carl questioned.

"He did some work for me," Dimitriov replied.

"What kind of work?" Carl asked. "Griffin already told us everything so there's no point from lying." Carl was fishing.

"I hired him to get me some fake documents for someone who needed them," Dimitriov said, knowing now that he had no other option but to come clean.

"Passports for who?" Dani jumped in.

"I don't know, someone called me asking if I knew someone who could have some passports made," Dimitriov continued.

"How much did they pay?" Carl asked.

"$30,000.00 each," Dimitriov offered.

"Who did Griffin get the passports from?" Carl questioned.

"I don't know," Dimitriov said.

"Who's Darkaoui to you?" Dani asked.

"I met him once in a club looking for weapons to buy. I work for the CIA." Dimitriov was trying to give the interrogation a different twist.

"We know that you cut a deal with the CIA to work for the agency in lieu of a life sentence, but you didn't keep your side of the bargain," Carl explained. "You have the weapons and you contacted Darkaoui for a payoff of $700 million dollars," Carl continued. "Where are the weapons?" Carl pressed Dimitriov.

"In a warehouse by the port," confessed Dimitriov.

"Where is the warehouse?" Dani wanted details.

"About two miles south of the port," Dimitriov replied.

"Is there a name or an address to this warehouse?" Dani continued.

"No, I don't know the name. It's just on a dirt road leading to the port entrance," Dimitriov added.

Carl gestured to Dani to step outside. They both walked out. Carl called James to let him know that they had Dimitriov and they know where the weapons are.

"This is the first good piece of *****news I got all day. Keep the son of a b***ch there," James ordered furiously.

"Now, we need to get to Darkaoui," Dani proposed.

"Not yet," Carl said. "Call Darkaoui and tell him we have the weapons and the delivery is scheduled for tomorrow. We need to keep playing his game," Carl continued.

Carl had more questions for Dimitriov, so he went back inside. "You said Griffin got you the fake passports through someone he knows. What's his name?" Carl asked.

"I don't know his name," Dimitriov replied.

"Stop the sh*t, give me a name," Carl yelled.

"I swear, I don't know his name," Dimitriov responded.

"Ask Griffin, I never met the guy. Griffin was the contact," Dimitriov added.

While Carl was pushing Dimitriov for answers, Dani went back to Griffin.

"What is the name of your contact for the fake passports?" he asked.

"Oleg," Griffin replied.

"Where do we find him?" Dani asked.

"I don't know," Griffin refused to give details.

Dani pulled a cell phone from his pocket and he ordered Griffin to call him.

"I don't have his number," Griffin lied.

"How did you get hold of him?" Dani put Griffin on the spot.

Griffin was confused by the question; he could barely make sense of what he was saying.

"What?" Dani said.

"Nothing, I don't have his number," Griffin insisted.

Dani stopped the questioning and decided to send another agent to Griffin's apartment to check for anything that might lead them to Oleg. Inside the apartment there was nothing unusual. Everything looked in place and there was no trace of evidence which showed a connection between Griffin and Oleg. After an hour searching every corner of the apartment, the agent called Dani to let him know that they couldn't find anything, when the unexpected happened. Taking a last walk before leaving the apartment, the agent noticed a dark spot very close to the dining room table. He walked to it, got on his knees to check it out and found what looked like a blood stain.

He called Dani again to tell him what he found. "Hey, Dani, I just noticed a blood stain near the dining room table right leg. I am not sure if this is the subject's blood or what," the agent announced.

For the next few days nothing happened. Carl and Dani did not meet with either Griffin or Dimitriov. Dimitriov and Griffin were kept in different cells. Eventually, they were formally charged; Griffin with counterfeiting and aiding document forgery and Dimitriov with counterfeiting, aiding illegal persons to obtain forged documents, and the biggest charge for Dimitriov, possession of a large quantity of illegal firearms.

Early on Tuesday morning, Dani showed up at Griffin's cell.

"You not only are charged with counterfeiting, but now you will be charged with the disappearance of Oleg Vokov," Dani had no proof but hoped that he could get Griffin to talk.

Griffin froze.

"What the hell I have to do with his disappearance? I want a lawyer!"

Right then, Dani knew Griffin had something to do with Oleg's disappearance.

"The blood stain in your apartment by the dining room is Oleg's, so a lawyer is not going to get you off," Dani said.

Griffin could no longer hide the truth. He sat there silent, looking at the ceiling as if he was asking for a miracle, but he knew that he was in way over his head. He ended up confessing to everything, including Oleg's murder. He told them where the body was. Adding to his charge now was murder. Griffin was going away for a very long time. As for Dimitriov, he was taken to where the weapons were and from there, he was shipped to a US military base at night. From the base, he would be shipped to the US to stand trial for treason, aiding terrorist groups to enter the US illegally and other charges that were to follow.

In boxes labeled as 'beauty supplies' and hidden behind crates of tools, no one would have suspected those boxes contained dangerous weapons. Several agents stormed the warehouse discreetly with no sirens or flashing lights and proceeded to climb behind the cranes and open the boxes one by one. Soon, a couple of trucks followed the raid; they loaded the boxes to move them to a secure location. At this time, Dani, as instructed by Carl, called Darkaoui to give him the news that the weapons were ready for delivery. However, Darkaoui, as a former secret agent wasn't going to take the chance of keeping his phone operational knowing that the CIA was probably tracking all his moves. He got rid of his phone. Dani knew that Darkaoui would have done so as well as no signal was transmitting from Darkaoui's location or communications. No one knew where Darkaoui was hiding.

Dani received a call from an unexpected number. The phone didn't show a caller ID or name. The screen just read 'unknown caller'.

At first Dani waited to answer, but after few rings he decided to pick up.

"Do you have my stuff?" Darkaoui asked

"Yes, where's Polina?" Dani interrupted Darkaoui.

"I want my supplies or my money back or the girl will die," Darkaoui threatened.

"Where should I deliver?" Dani asked

"I'll get back to you, leave your phone on!" Darkaoui instructed.

Darkaoui was calling from an undisclosed place in Europe. He travelled to Malta to deliver the fake passports to the people he hired who would use the weapons he bought from Dani. The next day Dani received a call directing him to where the weapons should be delivered. Darkaoui gave Dani precise directions to follow.

"I want the weapons to be delivered in two shipments to two different addresses."

Dani wasn't sure what Darkaoui had in mind but agreed to the deal.

"Once I receive confirmation the weapons have made it to the locations, I'll let the girl go." Darkaoui proposed.

The weapons were loaded in two different unmarked trucks. Dani was driving one and another agent drove the second. Carl stayed back. Before the weapons were loaded, tracking devices were placed on each weapon. The serial number and the type of weapon were recorded for reference. The two trucks headed out as planned.

While in route, Darkaoui called Dani, "Change of plans, drop everything at Location 1." He then hung up.

At the agreed location, Darkaoui was not there. Instead, three guys wearing black uniforms with their faces covered, with only their eyes showing, waited for the trucks to pull up. They waved them to a big bunker buried underground. The bunker was a half mile long with lights and a paved road. Inside the bunker were several rooms, probably used for meetings and terrorist operations planning. At the end of the bunker there was a room big enough to house all the weapons delivered. Dani looked at every inch of the bunker as he drove inside while making mental notes. The three escorts kept a close watch on the two trucks until they arrived at the destination. Dani's truck was unloaded; however, when the second truck driver got out of the truck and proceeded to help unload his truck, he was ordered to leave the weapons where they were. Dani tried to strike up a conversation with one of the guards.

"Where's Darkaoui?" he asked. The guard ignored him.

"I thought he was meeting us here," he continued.

The guard, still ignoring him, went straight to check if the weapons were all there as directed by Darkaoui. He took a long knife and started tearing apart some of the boxes, pulling out some of the arms and checking them closely.

Dani stood there watching the guard checking the weapons, then he pronounced, "I need to speak to Darkaoui."

The guard pulled out his phone and dialed Darkaoui's number.

"Kulu Tamam" (Arabic for everything is ok). He continued; "the delivery guy wants to speak to you."

"Put him on the phone" Darkaoui instructed his guard.

"I thought you were meeting us here," Dani said, frustrated.

"The remainder of your money will be transferred tonight," Darkaoui said.

"Where's Polina?" Dani questioned.

The phone went dead. A few seconds later the guard's phone rang again.

"Give him the girl," Darkaoui ordered.

The guard instructed Dani not to move while the second guard, with his weapon ready to fire, watched Dani closely. The guard disappeared for a moment and returned with Polina, her hands taped, and her face looked like she was roughed up little. Still she looked healthy, but she looked exhausted. The guard pushed her to Dani.

"Get out of here," he said.

Dani freed Polina's hands from the tape; they both got in the truck and headed towards the exit still followed by the guards.

"Did you get any information?" Dani asked.

"No, they blindfolded me, threw me in car and drove me here."

"Have you seen Darkaoui coming to this place?" he continued.

"I saw him once; he came in to tell me 'either your arms dealer delivers or you won't be leaving this bunker alive'," she replied.

"Did you hear from him?" she asked

"Yes, that's why we delivered the weapons here," Dani commented. "I have no idea where he called from, but I am sure he's aware of every move," Dani explained.

"I heard one of the guards mention Malta in a phone conversation," Polina revealed.

"You mean, Malta the country?" Dani asked.

"I guess so," Polina responded.

"Why Malta?" Dani wondered. "We arrested Dimitriov and his associate - some guy named Griffin," Dani told Polina.

"Who's this Griffin?" she asked.

"Some American citizen living in Kiev who spent time in a Ukrainian jail. He helped Dimitriov provide fake passports for Darkaoui," Dani said.

Driving away from the bunker, Dani called Carl to tell him that the weapons were delivered and Polina was free.

"Did you just hand them the weapons?" Polina asked, surprised. "What if they end up being used somewhere?"

Chapter 6

THE TRACKING

"We put tracking devices in every weapon," Dani explained. "We knew that Darkaoui's phone would not be easy to trace as he got rid of the one we were tracking. The best option to find him again and the weapons was to track the weapons."

"I never trusted that Dimitriov. He wasn't going to pass up such a big deal to make a buck," Polina said. "What's the plan now?" she asked.

"Carl wants to wait to arrest Darkaoui. He wants to use him to get to the people he works for," Dani replied. "Why Malta?" Dani asked again.

A couple of days later Dani and Polina landed in Ajruport Internazzjonali ta' Malta. It is a small airport with only one terminal. Why did Darkaoui chose Malta, Dani wondered. It seemed odd that Darkaoui would do business in Malta if the weapons were in Kiev. He kept going over in his mind all the questions that could explain Darkaoui's actions. Polina and Dani kept a low profile upon arrival in Malta.

They tried to avoid any suspicious activity that might attract the Maltese authorities' attention. As Dani and Polina were checking out every place in Malta where Darkaoui might surface, Carl was busy lining up a plan to get into the bunker to get rid of the guards and replace them with CIA agents so they would be delivering the weapons to where Darkaoui wanted them. On a Sunday night, a group of highly trained agents stormed the bunker and silently got rid of the guards. Among those agents there were two who spoke Arabic fluently. Carl had his plan well thought out. He did not want to raise any doubt in Darkaoui's mind that something was going on. After the operation he called Dani.

"The situation is under control", he said." Our people are driving the trucks to the place where the subject had instructed his people to deliver," he explained. Dani was little apprehensive at first, not knowing where the trucks were going to end up but after getting some details from Carl, he felt comfortable.

"What about the border crossing?" he asked.

"All paperwork is being done by the agency allowing the trucks to cross without any issues," Carl assured him.

After two days in Malta, Dani and Polina swept the entire region in hopes of seeing Darkaoui surface. Polina knew that Darkaoui was a party boy from the first meeting she had with him when they met at the Big Boy Club at the Rostok Palace of Culture, Harmatna. With his flashy clothes and money to burn, he craved attention and mingling with night club owners and patrons. She suggested to Dani to forget about searching aimlessly and try Paceville (St- Julian's) the main hub for nightlife. He agreed. In the evening they wandered from one club to another looking like average tourists seeking a fun time. Dani didn't drink but Polina would have a glass of wine or a martini. For a couple of nights nothing happened; they would spend an hour here and there going from one club to another, sitting down watching everyone that come through the doors, but no one looked like Darkaoui.

On a Saturday night they sat at Sky Club located on Dragonara Road in Paceville. They took a table not too far from the entrance facing the double doors. As usual, Dani ordered a sparkling water and Polina ordered a martini with a splash of vermouth. Soon after the waitress set their drinks on the table, Dani noticed three young guys making their way into the club. They were well dressed and clean shaven with their slick hair combed back. He kept following them as they moved through the club. Polina asked if he knew them.

"No, I have never seen them before," he replied.

The three were escorted by the club manager to a table away from the crowd. One of the young guys stuck his hand in his pocket and handed what looked like a bill to the manager. As soon as they sat down the manager rushed back to their table with a bottle of Black Label. Dani kept an eye on them. They sat there for a while, when suddenly, Darkaoui appeared, heading towards them. Dani and Polina kept their heads down. Darkaoui didn't pay attention to them; he walked straight to the table with the three guys. They stood, shook hands and sat down. Dani wanted to know what the conversation was about but had no way to listen. All he could see was a deep conversation going on with hands waving up and down, and Darkaoui pointing a finger at one of the three. Polina had a suggestion but was afraid Dani wouldn't be interested. She decided to share it anyway.

"I am curious to know what they are up to," Dani said, raising his glass of sparkling water. "I have an idea," Polina proposed.

"Sure, what are you thinking?" Dani replied.

"Why don't we ask the waitress to get closer to the table? Maybe she can hear something. It will be the easiest couple of hundred dollars she will get tonight."

"I am not sure she'll go for it," Dani responded.

"We have nothing to lose. I'll ask her," Polina proposed as she waived with a smile at the waitress standing at the counter.

"Yes, another martini?" the waitress asked.

"No, thank you, but I have a proposition for you. I will pay you $200 US dollars if you get closer to that table with the four guys and try to hear what they are talking about," Polina offered.

The waitress thought about Polina's offer for a minute, looked at the table, hesitating a little, then she agreed. $200 US dollars is a great pay day for few minutes work in Malta. Polina handed the money to the waitress who made her way through the crowd. She went to a table close to Darkaoui and his friends, pretending to wipe the tables nearby. She got to the adjoining table of Darkaoui, pulled out a new cloth and proceeded wiping the already clean table. Darkaoui looked at her; they exchanged a quick smile and he continued his discussion. The waitress spent a few seconds close by trying to listen and then returned to Dani and Polina's table.

"Sorry, I couldn't understand what they are talking about. They're speaking in a foreign language," she said.

"You didn't catch anything they were saying?" Polina asked, disappointed.

"No, but I noticed a paper on the table that had a drawn map on it," the waitress remembered. "I'm not sure if that helps. Sorry," the waitress apologized again.

Dani stepped outside to call Carl to tell him about the map. Time didn't matter; the call needed to be made whether it was early or late in Kiev. This was a race against what might happen, but he could not reach him. He did not leave a voice mail. The next day Carl returned Dani's phone call from a hotel in Malta. Dani's phone rung early in the morning

"Hello? "Dani answered the phone, half asleep.

"I saw your call," Carl said. "What's the latest?" Carl asked.

Dani sensed that Carl was not far away.

"Your voice is very clear, are you in Europe?" Dani wondered.

"Did you get any new information?" Carl asked. "I am in Malta."

"Where should we meet?" Dani proposed.

"Let's meet at the Pier in the main fishing harbor," Carl suggested.

At 8:00 am Carl and Dani met at the harbor.

"So, what's the story of the list of the countries?" Carl wanted to know.

"Polina slipped this waitress $200 dollars to get close to Darkaoui's table and try to hear what he and the other three people with him were talking about," Dani explained. "But the waitress couldn't understand what they were saying," she said they were speaking in a foreign language," he continued. "She did notice a map on the table."

Carl's suggestion to have the meeting at the pier was not just a coincidence.

"Let's take a walk," he offered to Dani. A few feet from the pier they came to a house on a hilly road. Carl entered a pin and unlocked the door. It was a safe house that the agency used as a secret location for its agents working in Europe and North Africa. "Having a safe house on the pier gives us easy access to different locations in Europe and North Africa," Carl said. Inside, Carl exposed some computers hidden behind a wall activated with a code as well as an arsenal of weapons. He logged in to the secure agency server and displayed the map on the screen showing where the weapons trucks were heading to.

"What are we doing about Darkaoui?" Dani asked.

"Nothing right now," Carl replied. "We need to follow him and his three guys to find out where they are staying," Carl said.

"Where's Polina?" he asked.

"She was going to check out the town today, from what she said last night. Maybe she can find out something new about the three guys that were with Darkaoui," Dani commented.

Carl kept his eyes on the computer screen following the trucks. "They are on A4 headed towards Strada Statale 738/E45 in Villa San Giovanni, Italy," Carl said to Dani.

"Are they going to Italy?" he asked.

"No, they are heading to Malta. That's why Darkaoui is here," Carl surmised.

"We have information that Darkaoui's intention is to ship some of those weapons to North Africa and parts of Europe. The fake US passports he got from Dimitriov were an easy way to move his people around since no country will suspect people carrying US passports. He knew that Kiev is a hub for any illegal activity from weapons to fake documents and that's why he was there."

"You and Polina should go back to the same club you saw Darkaoui. If they are there, follow them to find out where they are staying," Carl said. "Wherever they are staying might have information that can help us," Carl continued.

That same evening, Dani and Polina headed to the Sky Club as instructed by Carl.

"I met with Carl today," Dani said to Polina upon meeting up in the evening.

"Where?" she asked.

"He's in town and he called me for a meeting." Dani was careful not to divulge the meeting location. "He wants us to follow Darkaoui and his group to find out where they are staying," Dani shared with Polina.

They sat at the club for a while before giving up and deciding to leave; Darkaoui did not show. But as they made their way towards the exit, those three guys were coming in.

Dani grabbed Polina's arm and said "Wait. Those are the same guys from last night. Darkaoui must not be far."

They casually returned inside, found a table, sat down and waited. In less than 10 minutes Darkaoui showed all dressed up and looking like he was already drinking somewhere else. He could barely keep his balance. The wait for Darkaoui and his companions was almost two hours before they decided to leave the club. Followed by Dani and Polina from a distance, the four men jumped in a cab. Dani waived to another cab standing by. He and Polina followed Darkaoui's cab for about three miles when the cab pulled up to a villa with a large gate. The four got out, pay the cab driver and walked through the gate. From a distance, Dani and Polina waited in their cab. Dani asked the cab driver to turn around and drive them back to their hotel. Upon their arrival at the hotel, Dani called Carl to let him know where Darkaoui was staying. Carl did not say anything. The only communication between Carl and Dani was brief.

"I'll call James and let you know what the plan is," Carl said.

James was happy with the news that Darkaoui was on the radar again. He instructed Carl to get in the villa and find anything he could: names, addresses, and anything that would give James a good basis to build a stronger case with his superiors.

Invading Darkaoui's hide out was not going to be easy. Who knows what he might have there? He knew that he was wanted, and he was not going to take a chance to just leaving his place unsecured. Carl, Dani, and Polina had to figure out how to get in without Darkaoui suspecting anything. They convened in the safe house on the pier to draft a plan.

After discussing the plan a while, Dani proposed the three of them should break into the villa in the middle of the night and either arrest Darkaoui and his group or simply eliminate them. Polina agreed. Carl, however, had a different take. He wanted to search every corner of the villa to see if there was something that could lead them to who Darkaoui was working for. He told Dani and Polina to do a stakeout by the villa and wait for Darkaoui and his people to leave. Then, they would all enter the place. All three of them agreed on Carl's plan.

The next night they met again at the safe house, went over the plan again, loaded their weapons and headed to the villa at night. They found a street adjacent to the villa, pulled up and sat in the car waiting. At around 10:30 pm, Darkaoui and his guys left the villa. Carl and Dani walked up to the gate, jumped over it and walked outside the villa, avoiding the camera. Dani picked the front door lock after disabling the alarm system from outside. Polina stood guard in the car in case Darkaoui or one of his people came back.

Carl and Dani went through the entire villa room by room looking to find any clues but didn't find anything. Carl, once again with his experienced eye noticed something unusual: a picture frame that wasn't flush with the wall. The wall had a bulge that was pushing the frame out a bit. He went closer to the frame, lifted it and removed it from the hook. Behind it he saw an opening in the wall with a small door with a latch. He opened the latch to find a built-in storage space with shelves. Those shelves were packed with money, cocaine and papers. He checked the stash of cocaine, then pushed the money aside pulling out the papers. Those papers had names of people along with passports of different countries and locations. He asked Dani to take pictures of the everything. While both Carl and Dani were busy with their search, Polina saw a car pull up to the villa. She tried to alert Carl and Dani, but it was too late. She had to act. With quick thinking and hopeful that it was not Darkaoui's car, she got out pretending she was drunk and lost. The driver of the car got out and asked her if she was okay. She was relieved that it wasn't Darkaoui.

"Is everything ok?" The stranger asked

"Yessss," acting like she was drunk, she said, "I am lost, and my car is making a weird noise."

The stranger offered to help her. He started the car and said that everything seemed to be fine.

"You cannot drive in this state," he insisted. "Can I call a cab for you? I would give you a ride, but I am starting my night shift as a guard in that villa," pointing to Darkaoui's villa.

"No, I'll be fine," Polina said, trying to keep herself straight.

"Good night," the stranger said.

Polina got on her phone, calling Dani. "Someone is coming in, he said he's the guard," she said.

"Carl, we need to get out of here; they have a night guard, he's coming in. Polina just called."

Carl put everything back, hung the picture and turned the flashlights off. They had no time to get out. They hid in a room leaving the door cracked a little and guns drawn waiting to see the guard coming in. The guard opened the door and walked in, took his jacket off and went to the kitchen. Walking back with a glass in his hand he saw the room door slightly open. He sat his glass down and proceeded to check the room. He opened the door, turned the lights on, looked inside, turned around closed the door and left. Carl and Dani were both hiding in the wide closet. They waited for a few minutes and carefully walked out of the room, checking for the guard. They heard the TV on, looked in the living room and saw the guard eating with his feet up on an ottoman watching a popular detective series, LA Law.

While making their way out, Dani unintentionally bumped into a chair. He was quick to grab it before it fell, but the guard heard the noise. He muted the sound on the TV and got up to check on the noise. Carl and Dani rushed towards the doors and silently hid behind the dining room window curtains. The guard peeked into the hallway in the direction of the front door, then walked to the kitchen before he returned to his show. Carl and Dani slipped outside without the guard noticing them. They jumped the gate again and ran to the car. They left the area in a hurry. Dani seemed little nervous, while Carl was calm.

"Anything interesting from your search?" Polina asked.

Carl was silent but Dani replied, "not much - some papers, money and cocaine."

"Cocaine?" Polina said surprised.

"It sounds a little odd, this cocaine deal," Polina commented.

Suddenly, Carl said, "the names and locations in that built-in storage space have something to do with the cocaine."

"What do you mean?" Dani questioned.

"Think about it, Darkaoui is dealing with weapons and cocaine which he sells," Carl explained. "My priority is in understanding who he is supplying the weapons to." Carl said. "If we can find that out, we'll find out where he's dumping the drugs."

While Carl was talking, Dani was deep in thought reliving his past chasing Mansoor and his corrupt gangs. He also thought about Jane. All those memories put him in a state of revenge against Darkaoui. He didn't care if Darkaoui was a drug dealer, weapons reseller or a terrorist. All he saw in Darkaoui was someone making money at the expense of destroying people's lives. Carl and Polina could see the intensity and the sweat shining on Dani's face. Carl knew Dani very well and he could tell when something was not right. He wanted to ask him what was bothering him but Polina didn't know about Dani's past and Carl was smart enough not to say anything.

They got back to town, split up, and Carl called James immediately to debrief him on what happened at the villa. Dani and Polina headed to the safe house to dig some more through the information they had. The names were familiar. Some of them were Arab names and others sounded like they were from Southeast Asia. Carl and Dani knew what those names meant; they had lived through this same scenario before.

As soon as James's phone rang, he picked it up. He could see the call was coming from Carl's number.

"We found a storage place hidden behind a wall with some cocaine, cash, and a list of names and locations," Carl explained to James.

James' attention went straight to the list. "What list?" he asked anxiously.

"We couldn't tell much from the locations on the list, but the names are a mix of Arab origin and others from

Southeast Asia. I believe these are names of people with whom he exchanges drugs for weapons, then he resells the weapons to his connections."

"The son of a b**ch! He's not only an arms dealer, but a drug dealer too," James exclaimed. "Listen, I want this ass***** and you need to do whatever it takes to get him. Let me know every move he makes; I mean every move. By the way, what's happening with your guy Dani and the girl Polina?" James asked.

"They're here," Carl responded.

"Make sure that they don't screw up," James warned Carl. "I want Darkaoui; don't kill him if you can avoid it. We want him alive. I want him to sing." James was making sure Carl understood the priorities.

"James, thanks for taking care of those papers for the trucks to cross the borders," Carl said.

"No big deal," James replied. "We'll talk," he commented before hanging up the phone.

Carl got the message that James needed answers right away. The pressure was mounting, and James had never taken so much high blood pressure medication as he did with the Darkaoui case. Carl and Dani wanted to arrest Darkaoui as much as James did, but Carl had something else in mind. For him, arresting or even killing Darkaoui was not a problem.

He could do that anytime. His main target was whoever it was that Darkaoui reported to. For the next few days, all three of them followed Darkaoui and his companion's every move. They tracked them to restaurants, apartments they visited and bars where they hung out. So many late nights, cold sandwiches and coffee cups. The three would sometimes get a little bit agitated with each other from lack of sleep, especially Polina and Dani.

Chapter 7

THE EMOTIONAL CONFLICT

To resolve the tension, Carl would intervene, changing the conversation to some other topic. On the third night of their surveillance, Carl lost his temper when Polina was less than diplomatic and made a comment about the agency being screwed up. He took that criticism personally. He felt the comment was a criticism against the United States of America. After all, this was a matter of pride and patriotism. Hearing the comment coming from a working, but non-US born spy didn't help. Polina didn't know Carl very well and that was the first time she got to see him for his authentic self, when he told her that maybe the CIA should have never involved her in the case. Dani didn't say a word. He waited for the right time which came a day later when Carl was away and he explained to Polina that she needed to watch what she said in front of Carl about the agency or the US government, or the work of the agency. Carl is very committed to the agency.

"I have never met anyone who loves his job as much as Carl," Dani explained.

"Well, I'll stick by what I said," Polina insisting.

"Listen, I don't care what you think or say about the agency." Dani replied, clearly a little upset. "I just want to be done with this f*****g case and move on with my life. Just do me a favor, keep your Ukrainian upbringing style of talking to Carl under control. Do we understand each other?" he continued.

Polina, although not thrilled by Dani's speech, agreed to watch her mouth. She mumbled something quietly, and the only words Dani heard was "you Americans."

He let it go. He chose not to make a big deal out it.

The trucks were making good time on their way to Malta They were almost to Bologna, Italy. Carl was being updated on their movement very often as he was tracking their route from the GPS located in the safe house. The tracking devices on the trucks were state-of-the-art devices with very precise and live data. They could even pick up the smallest interference that occurred. A week now into the hunt and Darkaoui and his gang still hadn't made a wrong move. Darkaoui was calculating every action and knew any mistake might cost him everything he was planning, including losing his own life. However, Carl, Dani and Polina's luck changed sooner than they expected.

On a Saturday night while Darkaoui and his gang were having dinner at a fine dining restaurant known as De Mondion, located at The Xra Palace Relais & Chateaux Misrah il-Kunsill, Mdina, Carl, Dani and Polina happened to be in the area where they saw Darkaoui surfacing from the restaurant with a woman by his side. She was about 5'9" with a trim build.

Dani asked, "who is she?"

"He probably picked her up at the restaurant," Polina replied.

Carl was quiet. He slipped out from the car, went to the trunk and pulled out a camera and zoomed it right at the two, taking photos. A phone camera couldn't capture the detail at that distance, especially at night.

"Everyone is a suspect as far as I am concerned. We're not taking any chances." Carl announced.

Darkaoui and his acquaintance sat and talked in front of the restaurant for few minutes. Carl later did a quick search of the license plate and found out that the woman with Darkaoui was not just anyone. Her name was Leila Almasi, the daughter of an oil tycoon with investments all over the world. She studied in the UK where she graduated from Oxford University.

After graduating she went to work for her dad for few years before she decided to fly on her own. She spent great deal of time travelling between the US, Europe, and occasionally Asia. Her first encounter with Darkaoui was at a party. Her trip to Malta was no coincidence. She operated a very lucrative jewelry company. Italian gold is the new trend for Arab women in many Arab countries. Even though the Italian gold is not exceedingly high in quality, the engraved name 'made in Italy' made it all the rage. Leila was not interested in her dad's fortune. She took advantage of it as much as she could, but she had other plans for her future. She met Darkaoui in a party in Genova. Darkaoui was introduced as a businessman with clothing chains all over the world and she was introduced as the queen of modern jewelry. They spent some time at the party talking about their businesses and they even explored the possibility to do some deals together. Darkaoui left the party early and had not seen Leila since. They exchanged phone numbers but neither of them ever called the other until that evening when they met at the restaurant. Leila was meeting someone for dinner and Darkaoui was finalizing his plans with the other three members of his gang.

Seeing Darkaoui at the restaurant did not really move Leila. She acted very normal. After dinner, as she was walking out, he rushed to her from his table. They stepped outside and chatted for few minutes.

"This is a great restaurant", she said.

"Without a doubt. I come here at least three times a week when I am in town," Darkaoui replied.

"How's the jewelry business?" He asked

"It's going well," she briefly replied.

The conversation lasted a few minutes before her driver pulled up in a black SUV. It was totally blacked out from wheels to the top. The SUV looked like an armored military tank. The driver jumped out, opened the back door while slightly bowing to her. He looked like a body builder with a heavy and uneven body structure. The suit jacket seemed so tight on him that he could barely move his arms opening the door for her. The look on his face was traumatizing with 'mad as hell' facial lines. Carl could not see the driver's face but was able to take a clear photo of the license plate. The plate had a custom name, 'KWN1987'.

The SUV drove off and Darkaoui stood there lighting up a cigarette and watching the car leave. He seemed to be thinking about something. Carl, Dani and Polina kept watching him the entire time while he was standing there. He then walked back to the restaurant. Dani suggested following him inside but Darkaoui had already met him and Polina.

"That would be a major mistake," Carl said.

He volunteered to go in as Darkaoui had no idea what Carl looked like.

Inside the restaurant, Carl went to the bar, sat down and ordered a mineral water. The bartender wasn't thrilled by the order. He wasn't going to get a good tip on the water. He served it to Carl with a rather unpleasant air. Carl noticed but didn't say anything. He acted busy, looking at his phone while taking a quick glance every now and then around the restaurant so as not to attract any attention. He saw Darkaoui with his gang; they looked like they were in some kind of argument. Carl watched them for few minutes then pretended to head to the bathroom. Walking by Darkaoui's booth he stuck a tiny wireless microphone on the edge of the booth without Darkaoui or his companion's notice. The microphone was so small that it would be difficult for anyone to see it. He walked to the bathroom, walked back out and headed to the car. Dani and Polina were still in the car trying to figure out Darkaoui's plan. They were asking questions to which they had no answer. 'What are the weapons for? Why is he in Malta? Who's the woman he was with?'

Carl opened the back door, got in the car and started listening to Darkaoui's conversation. The three were in fact having an argument. Darkaoui was not happy because one of his men had bailed out on him. The young guy didn't want to go through with the plan of killing innocent people. Darkaoui was furious and threatened to make his life a living hell if he backed out. The guy insisted that he was out. The third guy tried to convince the young guy to stay on, bribing him with money and power. At one point during the discussion Darkaoui told him in angry tone of voice, "Get out! I never want to see you again! "The young guy left the meeting, rushing outside the restaurant knowing that Darkaoui wasn't going to forget about this.

Sure enough, few days later the kid was gone. No one knew what happened to him.

The weapons trucks made it to Malta as planned and Carl met with the undercover agents driving the trucks. The rendezvous took place outside town few kilometers from Malta. Dani and Polina stayed behind, keeping track of Darkaoui's every move. Carl directed the agents to deliver the trucks to Darkaoui, but he wanted to be part of the operation. He wanted to see Darkaoui face to face. Darkaoui received a call in the middle of night.

"We'll be in Malta in a couple of hours," one of the drivers said.

"Let me know when you arrive," Darkaoui replied.

That was the entire conversation.

Two hours later as planned, Darkaoui's phone rang again. "Where should we meet?" the driver asked.

"Pull up to the side of the road and wait," Darkaoui ordered.

They pulled to the side as directed. They were about a half kilometer from downtown Malta and now waited for further instructions. Darkaoui and his companions showed up as planned. He went straight to check the weapons in both trucks. Carl had already met with the drivers before they called Darkaoui. Carl was sitting in one of the trucks and kept looking at Darkaoui.

Darkaoui took a quick glance at Carl. He pulled one of the drivers aside and asked, "who is that guy?"

"He's one of ours," he replied. His name is Jay Olburg; known as the 'silencer'.

"Is he clean?" Darkaoui wondered.

"Yep, he's been with us for many years", the driver said.

Darkaoui went to Carl, looked at him closely and walked away.

"Where do you want this to be unloaded?" Carl asked.

"You come with me," Darkaoui ordered Carl. "You ride with me and my guy will ride with the driver," Darkaoui proposed.

Carl got out of the truck and got into Darkaoui's car. Darkaoui could smell something was not right but he couldn't prove it. They started driving towards the town of Mdina. It was a quiet town with castles and old history. In Mdina, Darkaoui had rented an abandoned house with a wine cellar. It was the ideal place for Darkaoui to hide anything he wanted there. No one would ever suspect a massive quantity of weapons was in their town. Carl was on his guard the entire drive. Not a word was said by Darkaoui. Occasionally he would check his rearview mirror to make sure the trucks were behind him.

Then, after a period of a complete silence, he said, "do you know Dimitriov?"

"No, never heard of him," Carl played ignorant.

"Does the name Polina ring a bell?" he asked again.

"No, no idea who this person is," Carl replied.

$Chapter\ 8$

THE GAME

At the wine cellar the trucks were unloaded with Darkaoui following every move. He directed his attention particularly to Carl. Once the shipments were off the trucks, the drivers walked out. Only Darkaoui and Carl stayed behind. At that moment, Darkaoui saw an opportunity to make sure Carl was clean. He pushed him against the wall, pulled his gun out and started searching Carl. Carl didn't resist. He played the game right along. Darkaoui found a gun on Carl.

He pointed his gun to Carl's head saying, "Who do you work for? What's your real name?" He repeated his questions.

"I have no idea what you're talking about. I was hired by your contacts to deliver the weapons."

Darkaoui wasn't buying the story until Carl said, "Do you think if I was working for someone else that I would have driven with your drivers all the way to Malta? I could have gotten rid of your guys the first chance I had, and I had plenty of them. What the hell is your problem?" Carl raised his voice, feeling he had Darkaoui.

Darkaoui extended his arm, handing Carl his gun and walking away without saying anything. Carl took a deep breath and straightened his shirt.

Outside, Carl gestured to the secret agent truck drivers. They already knew what Carl had in mind. Carl got in one of the trucks and drove off. Darkaoui had already left the place telling the drivers he would be in touch.

Carl and the agents made their way back to town, heading to the safe house on the pier. They split up before getting there; Carl went in first and the other two agents waited to make sure they were not followed before they went in.

Dani and Polina joined the meeting. Carl made the first introductions and immediately proceeded, detailing the plan. "The weapons are in Mdina in a wine cellar. Darkaoui is probably going to try to get them out as soon he gets a signal from the people he works for. We need to intercept him." Carl explained.

"How would we do that?" Dani asked. "He already knows that the weapons are there and he's probably on the phone trying to get them moved out as we speak," Dani continued.

"We have to arrest Darkaoui with the weapons," Polina jumped in. "This is the only way we can secure the weapons and put Darkaoui away," she offered.

"Wait a minute" one of the agents said," these weapons already have tracking devices on them, so we can locate them wherever they are. We should wait for him to make the move, find out where they are going to end up, then we can take over from there."

Carl listened then agreed with the plan. "Meanwhile, I want you to keep him in sight at all times. Every place he goes to, people he talks to, he goes to a bathroom- you follow him. I don't care where. We will be with him everywhere he goes."

The plan was now in full motion with Polina, Dani, and the other two agents circulating Malta, keeping an eye on Darkaoui and digging for any information on the weapons deal. Maybe someone is already in town to meet with Darkaoui. That same week, the 'Times of Malta' had the biggest story published on the front page, 'Young Man Found Strangled with A Bag Over His Head in an Alley.' The young guy's picture was on the front page. Carl saw it walking by a news stand; he stopped, read the headline 'Who Done It?' He grabbed a copy, paid for it and kept walking. He sat at nearby café shop and started reading the story. The face of the young guy was familiar. Carl recognized it as soon as he saw it. It was the same guy who refused to go along with Darkaoui's plan. The news of the dead kid was all over town. Some assumed it was a drug deal that went wrong, but others believed he was mugged and killed. Carl couldn't do anything to Darkaoui about the kid's murder because he had no jurisdiction in Malta. This was a case for the Maltese police. Carl needed clearance for Darkaoui's arrest, so he called James.

"Foster speaking," James answered the phone.

"It's me," Carl announced.

"What's the latest?" James asked right away.

"We need clearance to put Darkaoui away. I have enough evidence to go after him."

"Talk to me," James was impatient to hear the details and interrupted Carl.

"He killed one of the people working with him because the kid refused to go along with Darkaoui's plan for using the weapons. The 'Times of Malta' published the kid's picture on the front page. He was strangled in an alley last night."

"We cannot go by some kid dead in an alley to justify Darkaoui's arrest; this is an internal matter," James pushed back. "We need something solid," he continued.

"The only thing we have him for is the weapons, you understand that, the murder is not our problem," James said.

"Something else - the Brits are also involved in the Darkaoui's case," James mentioned. "They have their eyes on him, too," he added.

"Screw the Brits. I don't see any of them working here," Carl replied. "We must get this guy out of here before the Maltese government realizes what's going on," Carl said.

"Where are you planning on taking him? And what about the weapons?" James said.

"What's the closest US military base to Malta?" Carl proposed. "I can get the weapons out of here to a safer location until we put him on trial."

"You're kidding me," James said, raising his voice, "you want to get the US military involved in this?" he continued.

"I think it's better and safer having him in military custody until we ship him to the US to stand trial for the illegal weapons involvement," Carl said.

"Even if the Maltese authorities find out he has something to do with the kid's death, they won't charge him for the murder. They have no proof. He will walk," Carl explained.

James paused for a minute listening to Carl then said, "I am not sure if this is a good idea. If the word gets out that we are holding him at a military base, no US military base will be safe around the world. Too much of a risk to take."

The conversation between James and Carl did not lead to any action - for a while, that is. James needed to think about Carl's plan and Carl wanted to get to Darkaoui as soon as possible. Even though James was reluctant to agree with Carl, he decided to go with the plan. He called Carl later in the day to tell him it's a go but there was a slight change in the plan. James was against involving the US military from the start and he agreed to Carl's proposal only if Darkaoui was captured and kept somewhere in Malta until he could be extradited to the US. Carl met with Dani and Polina and the other agents to let them know that it was time to capture Darkaoui; keep him alive until he's shipped to the US for trial. They met at the safe house late in the evening to go through the final details of the plan. They knew where Darkaoui was from watching all his whereabouts.

That night, Darkaoui was celebrating his 45th birthday with his guests at one of the most famous and expensive hotels in Malta, the Westin Dragonara Resort located on Dragonara Road, Saint Julian's, Island of Malta STJ 3134 Malta. The Westin Dragonara has been the favorite destination for many wealthy people, government dignitaries, actresses and actors. Darkaoui's connections were all in high places and he could get anything done for a price. Money wasn't an issue for him, he had plenty of it from his illegal dealings. The tables were decorated with pure silk tablecloths and matching napkins. There were Waterford wine and champagne crystal glasses set to each side of some of the most expensive dinner plates money can buy - Versace's Prestige Gala Blue collection. Darkaoui insisted that his birthday party would be a historic one. Carl and Dani were planning on Darkaoui's lavish party to be the last one he would ever have. They needed to get him out of there without anyone knowing what was happening. Storming the party and taking him away was too obvious and too risky. They were sure they were not the only ones carrying guns. Darkaoui probably had his guards armed as well, and this was no place to exchange fire if something went wrong.

Dani thought about a plot to get to Darkaoui, but nothing seemed possible until Polina jumped in.

"I have an idea. What if we hire the same waitress-the one we paid $200 at the Sky Harbor Club- to seduce Darkaoui? She was willing to take the money at the club to get closer to his table to listen to his conversation with his guys. I think she'll do it," Polina explained.

Carl and Dani accepted Polina's idea since they had no other better option to get to Darkaoui.

A day before Darkaoui's party, Polina went to the Sky Harbor Club looking for the waitress. She sat at the counter and ordered her favorite martini. Halfway through her drink she saw Manwela Camilleri surfacing from the bar back entrance. She was on a smoke break.

They both looked each other with a nod and a smile, then Polina said, "Excuse me, do you remember me? I was here with a friend and we paid you some money to get closer to some guys sitting at that table," Polina said, pointing to the exact table.

"Oh, I remember," Manwela replied with a heavy accent. Her English was barely strong enough to communicate with Polina.

Polina invited her for a drink but Manwela declined, saying that she was on the job and couldn't drink. She grabbed a glass of water and Polina didn't waste any time telling Manwela, "I need a favor from you again, for which I will pay you."

"What kind of favor?" Manwela replied.

"My boyfriend is having his birthday party and I was told that he's cheating on me. I need to know if this is true or not." Polina explained.

"And what kind of favor do you need?" Manwela asked again.

"I need you to go to the party and seduce him. I want to make sure that I am not wasting my time with someone who cheats. I'll pay you $1,000 for your help," Polina mentioned the money to further entice Manwela.

"I don't know if I can. I have never done this before," Manwela resisted Polina's proposal.

"This is very important for me to know. Imagine if this was happening to you?" Polina insisted.

Manwela was silent for a minute, then said, "$2,000."

For her, $2,000 was double what she makes working almost two months that is if the bar is busy and her hours are not cut. Polina was little reluctant about Manwela coming back with a higher amount but agreed to the counteroffer.

"You give me half now and the rest at the party, okay?" Manwela said.

"I have $500 with me. I will give it to you now and the rest at the party, how's that?" Polina said.

After a little going back and forth, Manwela said, "Fine. No problem."

They both agreed to meet at the Resort the next day for the big celebration. Polina finished her second drink and left the club, heading there to meet with Carl and Dani. As soon she got out of the club, she called them to tell them Manwela was in. Carl and Dani made the final plan to be at the Westin Dragonara Resort ready for Manwela to move. The next day at 6:00pm they showed up to the hotel waiting for Manwela to arrive. They parked far away facing the resort entrance and keeping an eye on everyone who was showing up for the party. They were a little concerned that Manwela might have changed her mind. While they were trying to figure out something else in case Manwela didn't show up, they saw Darkaoui getting out of a limo with some other people.

Dani murmured, "enjoy the party you son of a b**ch."

A few minutes after Darkaoui made his way to the resort, they saw Manwela getting out a cab and before she got to the resort entrance Polina was standing next to her.

"Hi, Manwela," Polina said.

Carl and Dani stayed back while Polina and Manwela walked ahead. Polina wanted to explain to Manwela the plan for her so-called boyfriend Darkaoui.

"So, like we agreed, try to seduce him and I'll be close by to see what he does."

"How about my money? Do you have it?" Manwela asked.

"Yes, I do." She opened her purse and handed it to Manwela. Manwela stopped for a second to check if the amount was all there, stuck it in her had bag and they kept walking.

Manwela had tan skin with light blue eyes and light brown hair. She was about 5'9" with a slim body. Darkaoui was about to fall head over heels. They entered the resort; however, the problem was neither of them had an invitation to show at the reception room entrance. This detail totally eluded Polina, Carl and Dani. They needed to do some quick thinking or the whole plan would go up smoke.

Carl and Dani attempted to distract the heavy-set guard at the entrance of the reception room. "Hello gentlemen, your invitation please".

Dani stuck his hand in his inside jacket pocket looking for it and start searching in all his pockets. Carl pretended to be totally drunk telling Dani, "give him the invitation".

"I am still looking for it. Hang on." Dani replied.

"I knew you were going to forget it," Carl said to Dani.

"I am sure I grabbed it," he mumbled, still searching in his pockets.

"Would you please move aside," the bodyguard asked Carl and Dani as other guests were arriving.

"Did you find it?" Carl asked Dani with a drunk person's voice.

"No, can we just go in?" Dani asked the bodyguard.

"Sorry, not without the invitation," he replied.

"Let's go find it," Carl slurred.

Meanwhile, Polina and Manuela had already snuck in, disguised as members of the reception service staff.

Chapter 9

THE PARTY

As soon as they got in, Manwela stepped in the courtyard where people were in full swing party mode. Polina stepped back to a corner away from all eyes, her gun under her waitress vest ready for action. She was keeping Carl and Dani informed of the situation via a hidden wireless microphone in her vest lapel. Darkaoui had not joined the party yet; he had a room reserved at the resort. It took more than an hour before he showed up, already drunk. Manwela took a quick glance at Polina who gestured to her telling her 'that's him'.

Manwela strolled around the courtyard with her drink in her hand. She gave Darkaoui a quick look with a smile; he returned the salutations raising his glass of champagne. He kept her in sight while talking to some guests. Dinner was on the way and Darkaoui's table was already populated with the 'who's who'. Manwela sat at a table across from his. After dinner, the evening really started with music blasting from the speakers and the dance floor packed. This was the chance

Darkaoui was waiting for; he wanted to invite Manwela to share the dance floor with him. She accepted. Polina was watching and talking to Carl and Dani and she watched Darkaoui engage in a conversation with Manwela. They stayed on the dance floor for some time before they went to a table by the pool and sat down. Darkaoui asked her to have a drink with him which she accepted. He went to the bar and came back with two glasses of champagne. With his head already heavy from all the alcohol he had consumed, he was in no control of his words. He started talking about himself as usual, bragging about who he is, what he has and the people he knows. Manwela listened to him. He didn't even pay attention to the people who came to wish him a happy birthday. Manwela was his focus that evening. After an hour sitting at the table together, he decided to try his luck by inviting Manwela to go out with him.

She explained to him that she was married to a government official, but he insisted. Manwela resisted and said, "I'll be right back."

She pretended to head towards the ladies bathroom. Followed by Polina, they hid in a corner to talk.

"What was he saying to you?" Polina asked.

"He's totally drunk. He asked me to go out with him," Manwela replied.

"Did he say anything else?" Polina wanted to know more.

"He talked about who he is, what he has, the people he knows," Manwela shrugged.

"That's Darkaoui, all right, he always finds something about himself to say," Polina commented.

Around 11:30 pm the party started winding down and people were slowly leaving. Carl and Dani waited for the right moment to grab Darkaoui. Manwela pretended to wait for her chauffeur. Darkaoui offered to give her a ride but she told him her driver was already on the way. He insisted on waiting with her but Polina was ahead of him, calling Manwela on her cell phone.

"I need to take this call," Manwela said to Darkaoui.

She stepped away, walking towards the hotel lobby where a cab was already dispatched for Polina; it was waiting for her outside. She jumped in the cab and left.

Darkaoui waited for her to come back but after a while he gave up, went to the untended party bar, grabbed a bottle of hard liquor, poured himself a glass and walked towards the lobby heading to his room. Before he made it to the lobby, Carl was standing next to him. He pretended to be a little drunk and bumped into him, injecting him with a drug. Darkaoui was so drunk he didn't even realize it. Darkaoui looked at him and held on to the couch arm next to him before falling on to it.

The night shift receptionist rushed from behind the counter, asking, "Is he okay?"

"He's fine. We just had little too much to drink. It was his birthday. Can you do me a favor?" Carl asked the receptionist. "Would you unlock his room for me? I searched for his key in his pockets but didn't find it. I am sure he left it somewhere by the pool or on a table."

"What's his room number?" the receptionist asked. "I don't know," Carl replied.

"What's the name?" the receptionist asked.

"Darkaoui, Naim."

The receptionist found the reservation and said, "no problem."

They took the elevator to the 5th floor where the receptionist opened Darkaoui's room to let them in. But the receptionist was curious about where Carl was staying.

"Excuse me sir, are you a guest in our hotel?" he asked.

Carl paused for a second, then said. "No, I am in another hotel; your hotel was full when I called for a reservation."

"Very good," the receptionist's curiosity was satisfied.

Carl locked the door threw Darkaoui on the bed and started searching the room. Maybe he could find something. He searched everywhere but discovered nothing. The small safe was locked and there was no keypad or numbers on it; the code to open the safe was tied to a second special access card provided by the hotel. The card is given to guests when they check in and if any non-registered guest tries to use the card, the embedded chip will automatically recognize that and disable it. Carl found the card in Darkaoui's pocket and read the warning on the card. He pulled Darkaoui up, put his arm around his neck and dragged him to the safe, put the card in his hand while holding it firmly so he wouldn't drop it and stuck Darkaoui's hand against the safe. It opened. He threw him back on the bed and went to the safe. There were a few passports, a pile of different foreign currencies, a couple of fancy watches, a cell phone and a gun.

Polina kept watch on the front of the main entrance in case anyone suspicious showed up looking for Darkaoui, while Dani waited on the back side of the hotel with the car running. In the meantime, Carl, after taking only the passports and the cell phone, opened the door and took a quick look in the hallway. He didn't see anyone. He grabbed Darkaoui by his arms, pulling him up putting his arm around his neck, made his way to the emergency stairs towards the back-exit door. Going down the stairs, Darkaoui seemed to regain consciousness but not for long. He looked up at Carl and tried to fight his way out of Carl's grasp, but Carl knocked him out with a punch in the face. They put him in the car, picked up Polina and sped off. The plan was to take him to the safe house and contact James for further instructions. Sitting in the back with Polina on one side and Dani on the other side, Darkaoui was trapped between two guns. He had no way of escaping if he woke up. They arrived at the safe house where they put him in a dark room. Carl proceeded immediately to call James.

"We have Darkaoui in custody, what's the plan?" he asked.

"Get as much information from him as you can then we'll arrange for his extradition to stand trial," James explained. "Whatever you do, keep him alive. He's the only asset we have now," James continued.

None of the three slept that night. The pressure of having Darkaoui in a room in the safe house was too high to even consider sleep. They took turns dozing off for an hour each. Around 3 am they could hear Darkaoui speaking in Arabic; barely able to pronounce words clearly. He kept saying 'maya, maya' which Carl and Polina thought was some woman's name, but Dani understood Darkaoui was referring to 'water' in Arabic Egyptian. He needed water after drinking all that alcohol he consumed at the party and before. But asking for water was also an excuse for him to know who was behind his kidnapping. Dani opened the door holding a bottled water and handed it to him. Darkaoui saw Dani and remembered him from their first meeting.

"Who are you and why am I here?" Darkaoui asked.

"Here's your water." That's all Dani said before leaving and locking the door again.

Darkaoui, as smart as he was, realized that the situation had taken an unfortunate turn. As a trained secret agent, he could sense that this kidnapping was planned by government agents. He put all the pieces together from the first time he met Dani, Polina, Dimitriov and understood he was under arrest. He had to find a way to get out - but how? In a safe house surrounded by agents with guns and only one door, he figured there was no way to escape without being killed. He sat there the rest of the night plotting his breakout.

The time was now 6:45 am and Dani unlocked the door to check on him, but Darkaoui pretended to be asleep when he heard the door opening. Dani took a quick glance and closed the door. About an hour later he banged on the door asking to use the bathroom. Dani showed up to escort him to the bathroom. On the way, Darkaoui quickly scoped out the area, noticing two agents nearby. Carl and Polina were not there. He made a mental picture of what he saw and proceed to the bathroom. In the bathroom he looked around, checking drawers and the cabinet for something to use as a weapon but couldn't find anything. The only thing he found was toilet cleaner, and he decided to drink some of it. He felt sick and it got worse as he went back to his room.

He started yelling "Help, help!" with his hand pressing against his stomach.

Dani and the two agents rushed to the room to see him on the floor in agonizing pain. They tried to pick him up, but he would not move.

"I need a doctor, please help," he moaned.

But Dani thought he was playing a game until he saw foamy yellow stuff coming out of his mouth. "Shit!" Dani said, "get the car" he ordered the agents. "Where is Carl?" Dani asked.

"I haven't seen him," one of the agents replied.

"We need to get this piece of garbage to the hospital before he dies on us. Let's go," Dani continued.

They put him in the back of the car with the two agents and Dani drove. Carl and Polina went to a nearby restaurant to pick up some breakfast to bring back to the safe house for the rest of the team - even for Darkaoui. As soon they got the call from Dani, they left everything at the restaurant and were on route to the hospital. While Polina got behind the wheel, Carl was on the phone with Dani.

"What happened?" he asked.

"This ass*****must have done something to himself in the bathroom," Dani said.

"Listen, we need him alive, we can't lose him."

"See you at the hospital."

They drove him to St. James Capua Hospital. The 11-minute drive from the safe house to the hospital seemed like hours. Dani was afraid Darkaoui might just collapse in the car. At the hospital, a couple of nurses put him on a stretcher and sped towards the emergency room. Carl and Polina pulled up.

"Where is he?" Carl asked.

"They took him in," Dani said.

"We can't leave him alone," Carl commented.

"I tried but the nurse refused to let us go with him."

Carl ordered his agents to go stand by all exits. Polina parked the car in the front of the hospital facing the main entrance. Keeping an eye on the doors, the other two agents were directed to stand by the elevator door and the other by the back-emergency exit. Carl and Dani went to the second floor where Darkaoui was being treated. They stood in the hallway waiting. After about a half an hour the doctor showed up.

"He's in a bad shape. What happened to him?" The doctor asked

"We don't know," Carl replied briefly, not wanting to go into details.

"He has swallowed some chemical solution and it's all over his internal organs. We have cleaned most of it, but we don't know how much is left," the doctor explained.

"We have to keep him a day or two under observation," he continued.

Carl wasn't happy with the doctor's decision to keep Darkaoui in the hospital. At that point Carl had no choice, but to let the doctor know what the situation was.

"This is the United States Government and that man is under arrest. I need to keep my men by his room," Carl said, trying to convince the doctor to cooperate.

"This is a hospital with a good reputation and this man in under my treatment now. Until he is better, I am not having the US government stand guard in the hallway. You can do whatever with him once he's out of the hospital," the doctor replied with an annoyed tone. "If you'll excuse me, I have other patients to attend to," he continued before walking away.

A few minutes later Carl and Dani saw Darkaoui being taken to a recovery room down the hallway. They took few steps forward to see if he was awake, but he was out.

Chapter 10

THE ESCAPE

Carl, not wanting to take any risk with the mission, instructed the team to camp at the hospital for as long as it was going to take. Later that morning, Darkaoui was moved to a room across from the recovery station. Awake but a little drowsy, he was aware of everything around him. Later in the evening, at around 11:15 pm, right after the nurse finished her round checking on her patients, she came to see Darkaoui. He was the last one she checked on before turning in her report.

Dressed in some stolen clothes from another patient room, along with the patient's stolen cell phone, he somehow was able to sneak into another empty room without being seen by Carl's agents. A patient in that room was discharged during the day, and after cleaning it, the cleaning crew left the window cracked open a little to air out the room. Darkaoui forced the window wide open using all of his strength, made a rope with whatever sheets, towels, and bed cover he could find, tied it to the bed leg which he had rolled to the window wall, so it was firmly secured against the wall as an anchor. He climbed out lowering himself almost to the ground. The rope was a little too short to make it all the way down. He jumped, landing on his feet. He was now on the run. He had contacted one of the guys he was with at the restaurant and arranged to be picked up. The driver was waiting at the scheduled time. He got in the car and disappeared. Next day the morning nurse came in to check on him when Carl and Dani saw her rush out of the room in such a hurry. They thought something had happened to Darkaoui.

Carl ran towards her, "Is there a problem?" he asked.

"The patient is not there," she replied in panic.

"What do you mean, not there?" Dani questioned.

"He's not in the room: his chart says he will be here for two days," the nurse said.

Carl started swearing up a storm. Dani stood there not saying anything. There wasn't much to say. Darkaoui was gone and they had no idea where he had gone.

For weeks, the hunt was on to locate him. From coffee shops to hotels, restaurants and any other places they suspected they might find him or at least find some information to help them in the search. They showed his picture to every person they asked but no luck. As soon as

James heard the news, he could be heard screaming from his office.

"Where the hell were you all? You allowed him to escape?" he shouted at Carl.

"We were not allowed to approach his room," Carl explained.

"Damn these European countries," James muttered.

After a phone call to the US Embassy in Malta to arrange for a meeting with the Maltese head of secret service, a few hours later James boarded a plane to Malta to sort things out. The head of the Maltese secret service, Abram Galea, seemed a little apprehensive about the US government involvement in Malta. Abram Galea understood James' concerns and how dangerous Darkaoui was, but he was too stubborn to accept the need to work with the US authorities. He had deep concerns about allowing a foreign government to interfere in Maltese internal affairs. He was very clear with James.

"Give us the information your government has about this Darkaoui and we'll deal with it without your help," Galea stated.

James got the message that Abram was not going to cooperate on this matter. The meeting lasted half an hour and James was on his way out. He never told Abram that the agency already had CIA agents in Malta. The only information he shared with him was that the US government suspected that a terrorist who was planning attacks against US interests in Europe was believed to be in Malta or Italy.

"We're not going to get any help from the Maltese," he shared with Carl.

"You and your team are on your own to get this resolved. The agency will help in any way possible but if something goes wrong, sorry in advance," James commented.

Carl related James' latest information to Dani, Polina and the other agents. This was no surprise to any of them as the CIA's rules of engagement have always been known to any agent affiliated with it.

Weeks of searching for Darkaoui went by and there was no sign of him. Carl and Dani were frustrated that they lost him after they had him. They searched in every place they could think of; they even went back to the warehouse where the weapons were - but nothing. They figured he probably crossed into Italy or another country in Europe. All hopes of finding him again were starting to fade away. James left to go back to the US after his failed meeting with the Maltese secret services boss. He didn't see any reason for him to stay in Malta. With the four agents on their own now, the mission was more complicated than before because Darkaoui was out there and none of them knew what his next move would be. James's meeting with the MSS Chief will raise suspicions that the US government agents are already in Malta which will cause Carl, Dani, Polina and the other two agents to be exposed, and therefore jeopardize their mission. The situation was getting more complicated.

Polina on the other hand, was not too happy that Carl decided to slow things down. For her it was a matter of pride. She secretly thought that perhaps she could get the job done better than the male spies, especially after Carl told her that maybe the agency should have never brought her on. Even though she felt that way, she could not go against Carl's decision to wait. The next couple of days at the safe house they were back at the drawing board, going over all the information they had gathered about Darkaoui, trying to determine whether they missed something that could help them relocate him.

Dani said, "the only way to find him is to get to the guys who were with him at the club."

"I am sure MSS is watching us by now. We can't be picking up people without being noticed," one of the agents said.

"Hear me out," Dani replied, "these guys certainly know where Darkaoui is. If he's still in Malta, they must be in contact with him. If we can get to them, we'll get to Darkaoui. We'll find a way around the MSS," he continued.

Carl listened attentively to Dani's proposal and didn't seem to totally reject it. He knew that Dani could deliver if he believes in something. He has seen it before. He agreed to the plan.

Later in the evening, Carl and Dani went to the Sky Club looking for Darkaoui's guys. They arrived little early, each one going in different directions inside the club. They kept a close watch on the people coming and going but didn't see the people they were after. At around 9:45pm, as they were about to give up, they saw one of the two guys walk in and sit at the bar. Carl and Dani waited to see what happened next. Essa Said ordered a drink and was chatting with the girl sitting next to him. To Carl's and Dani surprise, the girl was Leila Al-Masi - who they saw talking to Darkaoui in front of the restaurant. They looked at each other from a distance, trying to understand why she was at the Sky Club at the same time as Darkaoui's guy. How do they know each other? The conversation between the two lasted for a while; they had a few drinks before they left the club. Carl and Dani followed them. Once outside, Said and Leila split up. Dani followed Said, and Carl was on Leila's trail, both Carl and Dani hoping that one of the two will lead them to Darkaoui's hiding place.

Halfway into the pursuit, Leila ditched Carl as she was very familiar with every street and alley in Valletta City. She hid in a dark narrow alley while Carl kept looking left and right trying to see where she disappeared.

Dani, in his pursuit, caught up to Said. He walked up and asked him for a lighter, looked him straight in face and as Said reached in his pocket, Dani grabbed him by his jacket collar pinning him to a pole. Said wasn't about to let Dani get the better of him. After a short wrestle between the two, Said punched Dani in the face and he freed himself. Dani lost his balance, letting go of Said, who took off running. Feeling a little disoriented, Dani held on to the pole, trying to regain his strength when he saw Carl walking back.

"What happened?" Carl asked Dani.

"I had him, but he got away," Dani said.

"Where is the girl?" he asked Carl.

"She disappeared before I could get to her. I lost her in the dark," Carl replied.

Essa Said spoke with a British accent and was so quick that Dani had no idea what happened to him during his altercation with Said. Carl and Dani headed back, both wondering what the relationship between Said and Leila was all about and why they left the club at the same time. The hunt now intensified for Darkaoui and this new detail about Said and Leila made the mission more tangled.

James had not had much contact with Carl since he left Malta. He was hoping that his agents would come out of this critical situation safe and that Darkaoui would be captured. However, he kept a low profile in case things took a different twist for Carl and his team. Darkaoui was gone and so were the two potential suspects that could have led Carl and Dani to Darkaoui. Amid all the confusion and frustration, Polina, a stubborn Ukrainian, had her doubts that Darkaoui had left Malta. She took off on her own, retracing every place previously explored for clues that might lead to a new discovery. As days passed, Carl and Dani were now convinced that Darkaoui had fled Malta, crossing to another European country. The new plan was now to go to Italy to look for him, but they had no idea where to start.

Contacting the Italian authorities would have had the same results as dealing with the Maltese government. There would be no help as the CIA did not have the best reputation in some European countries, including Italy. In 2009, an Italian court convicted the CIA base chief and 22 other Americans for kidnapping a terrorist suspect from the streets of Milan. Italy's government argued that the CIA cannot kidnap people from one country and try them in another country. This was a matter of sovereignty and pride. But even with this conflict of interest between the Americans and the Italians, Carl decided to exhaust every option possible. He arranged for a meeting with the Italians, hoping they were willing to looked past the trial and work with him. He met with Rome's police chief.

Anello Corrado, was a young guy in his 40's who was newly appointed as the head of the police. There were controversies surrounding his appointment to the largest police force in Italy due to his father's long-standing relationship with the Italian mob, but those controversies didn't matter much since the mob was pretty much dictating the rules. Corrado's arrogance was obvious as he met with Carl. It started with a cold handshake, and the discussion after that was more of an indirect attack against the US government. Carl played it cool, still hoping that Corrado would be helpful. After a 30-minute meeting going back and forth, Corrado made it clear to Carl that he was wasting his time in Italy. However, Carl wasn't wasting his time. His plan B was to work with the undercover CIA agents operating in Italy. He figured if the Italians were going to play hardball, he just had to go around them. After leaving Corrado's office, he met with one of the senior CIA agents who had operated in Italy for years.

Although he was an American originally from the Boston area, but with an Italian name, Agosti Paolo joined the CIA in his twenties. He was immediately sent to Italy for 15 years; he spoke fluent Italian and knew everything there was to know about the Italian culture from his Italian parents. During his time living in Italy, Paolo had made some very influential friends both in and outside mob organizations. Carl had never met Paolo before and had no previous engagement with him. It was through James that he got his contact number. Even though James was not fully invested in the case now, he was still informed about every move Carl and his team made.

Carl and Paolo's initial meeting was a debrief of the whole situation. They met at La Terrazza Restaurant on Via Ludovisi, 49 (Via Francesco Crispi), Rome, Latium. Carl offered to buy dinner. During the meeting he explained to Paolo why he was in Rome and what the mission was. Paolo, as a long-time spy in Italy, knew Carl would not get what he was after in Italy. He agreed with a mission to find Darkaoui if he was in fact in Italy. The search was now beyond Maltese borders. Dani, Polina and the other two agents were still scouting for any intelligence in Malta, and now Paolo, with the help of some connections was trying to find something for Carl in Italy. Said Esse and Leila Almasi had not surfaced since their encounter in the Sky Club. Maybe they were hiding somewhere waiting to hear from Darkaoui, the agents thought. Things were not headed in a very promising direction for Carl and his team. Nothing in Malta and no good news from Paolo.

"Hey, no one has seen this guy here," Paolo relayed to Carl. "I had some connections search for him, but no one has seen him or knows anything about him. The photo of the guy you gave me didn't do any good," he continued. All Carl could say was, "let me know if you come across anything."

Carl and the others were racing against time. James was waiting for answers and he would not allow this to drag on for a long time. He called Carl to let him know that if in few days if he doesn't have news on Darkaoui's whereabouts, he'll put another team on the case.

"I am being f*****g harassed by the people on the top floor. Why is the case taking so long to resolve?" James inquired.

Carl immediately told his team what James said to him. They did not like the sound of that, but they had to do get the job done before they heard again from James. If James said he will put another team on the job, they knew he would do it.

Chapter 11

THE MISTAKE

At the time when all hope for Carl and his agents of finding Darkaoui started dissipating, Darkaoui made the biggest mistake of his life. One night he infiltrated the warehouse where the weapons were and stole a semi-automatic gun. Polina's doubts were right. Darkaoui never left Malta. He was hiding in a secluded place rented under an assumed name. A place in the Island of Gozo, about an hour and half from the capital Valletta. He knew about Gozo from a previous trip he took there while in Malta. The island is surrounded by tall walls which gave Darkaoui a sense of protection and security. Darkaoui's 'faux pas' in going back to the warehouse and stealing the weapon was the misstep that Carl needed. The weapons were all encoded with tracking devices-which Darkaoui didn't know-and carrying the tracked weapon was like having the chip inside him. At first Carl figured someone had broken into the warehouse and stolen the weapons: it didn't cross his mind that Darkaoui was the one until he reviewed the recording from the camera that was secretly installed on the property. He could see Darkaoui breaking into the warehouse going through some boxes and packing a semi-automatic before leaving.

Carl was facing the computer screen and yelled, "we got him!"

Polina, Dani and the other agents rushed towards Carl.

"Let's go get him," Dani proposed.

"We should follow him first to find out where he's hiding," Polina suggested.

"That's exactly what we'll do," Carl announced.

They got in the car and followed the tracking device signal sending them in the direction of Route 7 leading to Gozo. At around 9:30 pm, they decided it was time to invade Darkaoui's hideout and bring him out. They split up to make sure that all sides of his place were covered in case he tried to flee. Darkaoui was sitting in his living room with his phone and his semi-automatic on the coffee table. He had food containers and a beer can on the table as well, which he had picked up on his way back. First, Dani quickly peeked in the window to confirm that Darkaoui was alone. Carl and another agent stayed in the front waiting for Dani to give them the go ahead. Carl and the agent forced the door open, at which point Darkaoui grabbed his machine gun and started shooting at them. Carl escaped the shooting, but his agent got shot in the chest, falling at the doorstep. He was dead. Dani and Polina and the other agent came running, each taking a position by the door and the side window. After a few shots, Carl hit Darkaoui in the shoulder which made him drop his weapon. Dani ran towards him, pushing the semi-automatic weapon away from him and pointing his gun at Darkaoui's head. Darkaoui didn't seem to take what just happened seriously; he started laughing and repeating to Dani, "are you going to shoot? Are you going to shoot? I knew you were no arms dealer when I first met you. I should've killed you and the other mole (referring to Polina) when I had the chance."

Finally, Darkaoui was apprehended but there was one thing Carl did not expect. He did not expect to see Leila Al-Masi and Said Essa standing in front of him in Darkaoui's hideout. Carl, Dani, Polina and the other agent, with their guns still drawn toward Darkaoui, could not connect the dots together. Why was Leila there and how did she know about the sting? Flashing their badges, Leila and Said pronounced, "MI6 agents here. He's our prisoner."

Carl, Dani and Polina looked at each other, not knowing what to make of this last turn of events. They had been sure Leila and Said were part of Darkaoui's gang but were surprised to learn otherwise. An argument erupted between all of them as to who should have Darkaoui in custody.

"We were after him for some time now," Leila said.

"He's in the US government's custody," Carl replied.

"There's no way you're going to have him," Leila commented. "This is our case. He'll be extradited and stand trial in Great Britain," she continued.

The discussion was between Carl and Leila only. Neither Dani nor Said or Polina could intervene. The tension rose between the two and it was clear neither of them was going to give in. They stayed there for some time going back and forth when Carl decided to finally call James to put an end to the conflict.

"Foster, here." He always answers the phone.

"We have a problem. We have the subject but there are MI6 agents here claiming that they should have him extradited to England."

"I told you the Brits were there also," James said. "Put them on the phone."

"This is Leila Almasi," she said.

"James Foster here. This is a matter of national security and we want to bring him to the US to stand trial."

"The British government will not allow that as the subject was first wanted in England," she abruptly replied

"He's not going to England, that's for sure. The US government will do everything to bring him to the US to stand trial."

The phone call ended with that message, and she handed the phone back to Carl.

"Make sure she doesn't mess up the plan." James warned Carl.

Leila Almasi also called her boss to let him know what was going on. He instructed her to stay with the subject and not to give in to the US pressure. An exchange of heated debates was happening between the two agencies, the CIA and MI6. The situation escalated to the point where now the CIA Director, Price William (known by his employees as Willie) and the boss of the British Foreign Intelligence service were disagreeing about who should have Darkaoui. The situation has become a tense one with each party flexing their political muscles to be in charge.

The drama continued between the two countries. Darkaoui was taken to Mdina with both the US and the Brits agents following each other closely. Carl, Leila and the others were waiting to hear what would happen next. Either the US government will take charge, or the Brits will take him in.

Carl didn't want to take him to the safe house from fear of exposing the US secret operations to another foreign country. The abandoned house in the Mdina that Darkaoui rented was a better way for Carl to keep the Brits away from the US secret business. For two days no news came either from James or the British government but by the third day something unexpected happened. Leila received a call instructing her that Darkaoui is now the US's government problem. She was furious by the unexpected decision to the point where she felt like killing Darkaoui and ending the story right there, but she didn't. She couldn't find anything to say except to tell Said, "We're done here. They can have him. We're out of here," she gestured to her colleague.

Carl wasn't surprised. He knew Darkaoui would end up in the US to stand trial. Or so he thought. Darkaoui's connections were too powerful to allow either the US government or the Brits to seize him. As cocky as he was, he did not show any fear from being extradited to either the US or Britain for trial.

On the very same night Carl, Dani, Polina woke up to a loud noise outside. A wall was blown out and Darkaoui was gone.

They rushed in every direction looking for him, but he was long gone. The mercenaries who came to liberate him knew exactly where to hit. Carl, Dani and the others were outraged that Darkaoui was once again gone. The first thought that came to Dani's mind was that the Brits had done it. Leila knew where the place was, and MI6 agents are well trained to pull off something like this. No one else would have thought of even getting close to the place.

Carl, on the other hand, had his doubts that this was an MI6 operation. He paused for a minute thinking, and said to Dani, "This is not MI6; it must be the people he works for. MI6 would not blow up a wall. They have other ways."

The four of them were pacing around wondering what had just happened. One minute Carl was making plans to get Darkaoui to the US and another minute Darkaoui was gone. Later that evening Carl received a phone call. No ID or name, no caller ID displayed on the screen. For a moment Carl thought DC must have heard the news about Darkaoui's disappearance and someone was calling to raise hell. He waited for a second before answering, trying to gather his thoughts on how he would handle the call.

"Hooper here," he answered.

"Mr. Hooper, we assume by now you know who you are dealing with. We can hit anywhere we want. There's no force that can stand in our way."

"Who is this?" Carl asked.

"It's not important who this is. What is more important is that you tell your government not to interfere in other countries' political fights. Your government does not understand what's at stake."

Chapter 12

THE MESSAGE

"Your government or any other western government is no match for what we can do. Your country may be the most powerful country in the world, but that doesn't scare us a bit. We have mastered ways to get in your government's head and we will keep hitting every one of your targets no matter where they are or how protected they are. I hope you make this message clear to your superiors. Good-bye Mr. Hooper," the call ended.

"Wait, wait," Carl tried to keep the conversation going so that maybe he could figure out who this guy was. Carl's concern wasn't so much who the person was because he knew that this person sooner or later would resurface in person or with another message, his concern was what the caller said.

They can hit anywhere at any time. Carl had no doubt that what he heard could very well be true. He shared with his agents what just happened.

With Darkaoui gone, the risks of an attack happening in any part of the world where the US has a presence are now greater than before. Darkaoui being arrested and kept alive even for a short time was a protection for the US against any attempt to attack because he wasn't just an international weapons dealer, he was also the leader of, 'The Reformists'. Their job was to create political and economic chaos in countries run by long standing government leaders. The Reformists wanted to change the governing system, giving them legitimate power to take over the governments and build economic wealth for an elite group.

The Reformists became powerful under Darkaoui's leadership; the terrorist group members spread to many countries and Darkaoui knew exactly who he needed in the group to make it just the way he wanted it, strong and efficient. He didn't go after the average person, he recruited only the brightest of the bright: scientists, politicians, doctors, engineers, scholars and others. Himself a graduate from Oxford University and very smart, he needed people he could count on to get the job done. For Darkaoui, this wasn't just a simple operation but a mission that required specific intellectual power if it was to be executed. Darkaoui's interest was not in a religious overhaul of societies, nor was he trying to create extreme religious groups to bring about change. His intent was purely political and financial. Most of the countries that were on his list of targets were rich oil Arab countries struggling for political and economic domination. Most of those existing political regimes were shielded by the US government and other western governments in exchange for foreign investments. The Reformists group's motivation was not necessarily to change the US's protection but to be the ones benefiting from it. By late 2000, the Reformists had gained major support of many misled Arab people, mostly young and uneducated individuals who believed that the group was going to bring them the economic prosperity they waited so long for.

The problem now facing Carl, Dani and Polina was much bigger than just finding Darkaoui. They were up against a cell and they had no idea how far it extended or who was in it. The three were trapped in a situation that had no solution in sight. Carl was under the gun by James to deliver Darkaoui to the US government, but now that Darkaoui was gone, and considering the phone call Carl received, these events created an even bigger problem to tackle.

Who are these people and where are they? He wanted to know.

As Carl was trying to figure out a way to put all the pieces together, thinking maybe something he missed would emerge, things could not have gotten any worse. Carl received a wire that a US diplomat, his assistant and two bodyguards stationed in Turkey were kidnapped on their way to a cultural event held in the convention center located on Harbiye 34267, Istanbul, Turkey. Now Carl understood that when the caller told him they can hit anywhere, he meant it. Whoever staged the kidnapping of the US diplomat had done his homework. But why in Turkey, Carl wondered? They could've done it in another country, but why Turkey?

Turkey was the right place for Darkaoui and his followers to hit because the Reformists wanted to create chaos in different countries, giving them an opportunity to build wealth selling weapons to various groups who were struggling for political power. The conflict between the Kurds and the Turks gave Darkaoui a huge opportunity to make it his mission to get back at the US government. The Kurds wanted their political independence from Turkey, and the Kurdish Nationalist Party referred to as the Kurdish rebellion had a long-standing conflict with the Turkish government, fighting for its political separation- but the US was never on board for the Kurdish independence. The opposition was based on the opinion that the time wasn't right for it. Kurdish leaders saw this as a lack of respect for their own sovereignty. The US stand on the Turks-Kurds conflict was a chance for Darkaoui and the Reformists to settle the score with the US government.

Kidnapping the US diplomat in Turkey was not expected by the US as government since the focus was more on other areas of the world where there was far greater danger to US interests; Afghanistan, Iraq, and other parts of the Middle East, Africa, and even Asia and Europe. But the Reformists had planned it so well that the US government totally missed the signs.

Darkaoui was once again in charge of calling the shots. After Carl received the news, he got on the first flight to Ankara leaving behind Dani and Polina. He wanted them to stay and monitor the situation in case something else came up. He walked to the heavily guarded US Embassy to meet with the US secret service boss to discuss the diplomat kidnapping case. By that time, the State Department was demanding quick answers. The only lead Carl and the secret service had was the stranger's phone call to Carl, but that lead was not going to help them in any way since they didn't know who the caller was or where he called from. Tensions rose between the different US governmental parties - the State Department, the CIA - and the Turkish government. Each one blamed the other for what happened. The State department felt the CIA fell short in their job protecting their diplomat and his staff; the CIA blamed the bureau for not providing enough information earlier about the Reformists and Darkaoui, and the Turkish government blamed the US government for putting Turkey's stability at risk by not sharing information about the Reformists group with Turkish authorities. The Kurdish rebellions didn't have a stronghold in Turkey until members of the Reformist group came into the picture in Turkey to train Kurdish rebellion members, now with Darkaoui leading the new movement.

Chapter 13

THE MOVEMENTS

At first there were some disagreements between Darkaoui and the leader of the Turkish rebellions, but as the two could not agree on who was in charge, a deal was made to have Darkaoui control the handling of any US intelligence movement in Turkey, since he was a former Egyptian secret service trained in the US. The other reason for not allowing him to lead the entire operation between the Reformist and the Turkish rebellions was because he was an outsider and this conflict concerned only the Kurds and Turks. However, Darkaoui wasn't going to just accept the agreement without any conditions. He wanted to strike a new deal with the Kurds of Iraq after the mission in Turkey was done. He demanded that the Kurds of Iraq had to allow him to bring in some of his Reformists to stage military operations in Iraq to overthrow the Iraqi regime. His intention was to create chaos in Iraq between the Kurds and Iraqis so he could supply the Iraqi Kurds with weapons. He knew they were ready to rise up against the Iraqi government but couldn't do it alone.

Darkaoui had scouted the situation before with the Kurds in Iraq and knew that plenty of money and power was waiting for him there. His deal with the Kurdish rebellion group in Turkey got him closer to his goal. The rebellion group agreed to his condition so long as he leaves Turkey as soon as the mission is done.

Carl, on the other hand, was increasingly worried as days went by, not knowing what happened to the US diplomat and his staff. With the pressure from his superiors and the US government pounding on him from every direction, for a moment he gave up hope that he would ever find the solution. He was in constant contact with Dani and Polina, thinking maybe something would surface in Malta that would help him get somewhere in Turkey, but nothing had surfaced. For few days no one knew where Darkaoui was or how to get to him. Then the unexpected happened. James called.

"Any new leads in Turkey?" James asked.

"Unfortunately, nothing," Carl replied with an exhausted voice. Dany and Polina are keeping an eye out in Malta, maybe something will turn up there that can help us in Turkey," he continued.

James paused for a minute while listening to Carl.

"This situation has gone way too far, and we cannot let it go any further," he announced. "I was told that someone else is involved in Turkey, trying to find out where the subject is. I am not sure yet who is involved but wait for instructions." James ended the call.

Although Carl did not really push to know who else was there, he was curious who else might be involved. He decided to just wait to hear back from James. Three days passed and no call came. He figured maybe things had changed and whoever was supposed to be in Turkey didn't make it. On Tuesday evening while having dinner at Turk Art Terrace Restaurant, located on Cankurtaran, Tevkifhane Sk. No:12, 34122 Fatih/İstanbul, the waiter approached his table and handed him an envelope. Inside was a note saying, 'meet me at the public square.' Carl didn't even think twice, leaving with most of his dinner untouched. He paid the waiter and left. The waiter tried to ask him if he wanted the food to go, but Carl shook his head. The waiter shrugged, surprised but started to clear the table.

Carl made his way to the public square as fast as he could walk. The square was a few blocks away from the restaurant. Twenty minutes later he was standing at the square not knowing what to expect. He had his gun ready in case something went wrong but was hoping that he wouldn't have to use it. He stood there looking in every direction of the square to spot who was going to show up. About five minutes later he saw someone walking towards him. He pulled his gun out of his holster and stuck it in his coat pocket, ready to fire. The person kept walking towards Carl and stopped few feet away. It was Leila Al-Masi, the British spy. Carl looked at her, a little confused.

"What are you doing here?" he asked.

"Apparently, for some reason you Americans are convinced that you can find a solution to any problem, but you can't." She was sarcastic but she meant what she said.

"You still haven't told me why you're here," Carl pressed.

"Same reason you're here, looking for Darkaoui," she replied.

"I thought the Brits were off this case since it is a US problem," Carl ventured.

"Your government decided it was time for the British government to come to the rescue," keeping her sarcastic tone, which Carl was not appreciating any more.

"What do you mean 'to the rescue'?" he asked.

"We know Europe better than the Americans do and if the subject must be apprehended, the British government is in a better place to do that."

Carl wanted to walk away but resisted the urge to do so because he remembered what James told him: 'someone else is in Turkey looking for the subject'.

"Back up little - is your government planning on taking the subject to England?" Carl asked.

"I don't know what the specific plan is," Leila said. "All I am aware of is that your government is in talks with the British government regarding the subject," she explained.

Carl was not sure if what he was hearing was the truth, but if Leila was right there standing in front of him then he believed she had credible information about the deal.

"What is your plan?" Carl asked.

"We know that the subject is not alone in Turkey. He has a group of followers called the Reformists who are probably working with the Kurdish rebellion group".

"We already knew that," Carl interrupted her. "How are you planning on getting to the subject?" he asked.

"We know from our sources that's he's been talking to the Kurds in Iraq, trying to sell them weapons for their military operations against the Iraqi regime. We also have information that he made an agreement with the leader of the Kurdish rebellion group that after his job is done in Turkey. He agreed with the KRL that he will bring the Reformists to

Iraq to form an alliance with the Iraqi Kurds against the Iraqi government." Leila explained.

"How do you know this information?" Carl asked.

Leila smiled. "I told you we know Europe and the region better than Americans," refusing to go into details. "The subject was seen in Istanbul 72 hours ago, speaking with someone."

"Do we know who this person is?" Carl asked.

"From our intelligence we know that his name is Agit Bejar, a former member of a group of Kurdish guerilla forces known as 'Peshmerga'," Leila replied. "He was the mastermind behind the operation that led to the arrest and killing of Iraqi soldiers at a check point controlled by the Pershmerga. It was a payback for the Iraqi government isolating the Peshmerga from fighting against Al-Qaida and Shia militia and replacing them with Iraqi Shia soldiers," she continued.

Carl had no other choice at this point, but to accept he would have to collaborate with the Brits. He didn't like the idea very much, especially after Leila made sarcastic comments about the US government. He was a proud US secret agent.

Leila's plan was to focus now on Agit Bejar if they wanted to find Darkaoui. The only way to get to the subject is first locating where Bejar is, she told Carl. "The subject is not an easy target to find as you know. He knows the spy business; he was one before, so I am sure he's being careful with every move he makes,"

"This guy, Bejar, where do we find him?" Carl asked.

"He's an addicted gambler. He usually shows up late at night in hotels and casinos reserved for high rollers only. We know that he does not just gamble, but also talks to certain people involved in illegal weapons and narcotics," she said.

"If your government had all this information why didn't you arrest him?" Carl asked.

"He was arrested by Turkish authorities several times, but always managed to be back on the street a day or two later," she replied.

"Someone is protecting this guy if he was arrested several times and released," Carl thought out loud, "and whoever is protecting the subject is also protecting this Bejar," he continued.

"Our goal is not to just go after him; we are more interested in who he works for," Leila commented.

Carl had a hunch who might be protecting the two based the phone call he received from the stranger, but didn't want to share that with Leila, just like she didn't want to share with him who her sources were for all the information she had.

Leila asked Carl to walk with her. Not too far from the public square a blacked-out SUV was parked with the only the fog lights on. She opened the door and they both got in. The driver did not even turn his head; he continued looking straight forward. She pulled out her laptop and the USB she had in a tiny hidden opening in her gun holster. She pulled up some video footage of the subject and Bejar, which was taken when the two met in Istanbul. She also had another video of Bejar from the casinos and hotels where he hangs out.

After his conversation with Leila, Carl concluded that the weapons Darkaoui had were probably making their way to Turkey to be handed over to the Kurdish rebellion group. They sat in the car for a while, going over those videos and trying to figure out why the two were at the public square.

Darkaoui did not really know Bejar. He met him through the Kurdish rebellion leader. Bejar was the deal maker between the Kurdish rebellion in Turkey and the Kurdish guerilla group in Iraq and Darkaoui. The Kurdish rebellion leader didn't want to take any chances dealing directly with Darkaoui on any operations in Turkey or anywhere else. He brought in Bejar to handle all dealings with the subject. Bejar's long standing work with the Kurdish guerilla group in Iraq had won him a reputation as a feared negotiator. He was even nicknamed the 'beast of the orient'. Bejar had his way of doing business. He either gets his own way when negotiating a deal or the person dies. No other way. The Kurdish rebellion leader knew that about him and that's why he hired him.

Darkaoui could not deliver the weapons he had because they were now in the custody of the US Secret Service and were being transported to a US military base in Italy. The Italian government was already made aware that a shipment of US weapons was headed to a US military base in Italy. All the documents were in place to authenticate the shipment as coming from Germany to Italy. Neither the Italians nor the Maltese needed to know that the weapons were hidden in their backyard.

Carl ordered both Danny and Polina to remain in Malta for some time just in case something surfaced that might help them in their mission. Dani was little reluctant to follow the order as he wanted to have a part in capturing Darkaoui. For him, Darkaoui and his kind were a personal affair from his first mission with Messoud and the killing of Jane. His entire life was turned upside down and he was not willing to just sit back and wait. He tried to convince Carl to allow him to join him in Turkey, but Carl insisted that Dani remain in Malta until the weapons were shipped to Italy. He trusted him more than anyone else.

Now the hunt for Bejar was on. Carl and Leila were searching hotels and casinos disguised as gamblers: Mr. and Mrs. Demir, Asli and Omer. With fake IDs and invitations, they had no problem getting inside some of the most expensive and luxurious private gambling places Turkey had to offer. There was nothing like them in Europe. The rooms were furnished with handmade furniture engraved with gold insets in the chairs and tables, the Isfahan Authentic Persian hand knotted wool & silk area rugs giving each room an elegant feel. Everything reflected the golden time of the Ottoman Empire, even the plates and glasses. These casinos were designed to cater to the rich and powerful. No one would have ever suspected such secret places existed in Turkey.

At the door Carl and Leila were each greeted with a cup of tea served in a 24Kt gold teapot known as 'Ibrik'. Even the teacup was made out pure crystal. The mahogany counter bar with Turkish mahogany columns were engraved and on which crystal shelves displayed some of the most expensive and rare bottles of alcohol. The counter and columns were layered with pure gold and even the footrest was made of gold.

Inside, Carl and Leila started checking every inch of space of the vast place; maybe they would see Bejar or even Darkaoui. People were totally immersed at their tables gambling. Smoke from cigars and cigarettes filled the air, but nobody minded that; it's part of the gambling atmosphere, it seemed. They split up to sit at different tables, betting money. Leila went to a roulette table and Carl to a blackjack one, but neither of them was lucky enough to win big. They lost money from the start and after trying few times to at least walk away with one win, they gave up. They decided to call it quits. They walked around separately, hoping to run into Bejar or see him walking in but nothing happened. Almost an hour later in the casino, they figured nothing was going to develop that evening. Carl headed to the coat check counter to retrieve their coats and prepare to leave.

While Leila was waiting, something strange happened. She heard some yelling in the bar and at first, she didn't give it much thought, but then she heard the name 'Bejar'. That attracted her attention to the conversation. She tried to listen in, but it was difficult to understand the language. She waited for Carl to come back.

"You see those two guys on your left at the bar?" she asked. "Don't turn around," she continued.

Carl looked at them briefly from the corner of his eye. "What about them?" he asked.

"I just heard them saying the name 'Bejar' as I was walking by them."

"Do you think they are referring to the same guy?" Carl asked.

"I am not sure; I could not understand everything they were saying but I heard his name thrown in the conversation."

"Maybe it's someone else," Carl said.

"I have a feeling that the conversation has something to do with him," Leila insisted. "Let's wait!" she proposed.

Carl put the coats on one of the chairs when soon, one of the employees rushed towards him. The employee was indirectly telling Carl that this is not a place where you leave your coats on chairs.

"Would you like me to check your coats for you sir?"

"Thank you, we're leaving soon" Carl replied, but Leila jumped in, interrupting him saying, "Yes, please. Thank you!"

"I thought we were done here," he said with an annoyed voice.

The two guys sat at the bar for a while, engaged in a long discussion. Leila and Carl kept them in their sights. Not long after, they saw Bejar walk in with his bodyguards like he owned the place. He was greeted from far away by the casino employees and other guests and shaking hands with others. Leila and Carl moved away, standing in a corner contemplating their plan.

"This is him, Agit Bejar," Leila said to Carl.

"Let's go lose some more money, but first let's see which table he's going to play at," she continued.

Bejar had a reserved seat at every table, but his favorite one was the blackjack table. He took his seat, gestured to the waitress who brought him a drink. He was a hard liquor guy and Amaretto Sangria was his drink. The waitress knew that. She brought him his drink and placed it on a coaster. He took one sip and gave a satisfied nod. He made small talk with the table dealer, making a joke here and there. Leila and Carl had to get closer to Bejar.

"How do you want to do this?" Leila asked Carl.

"We need to get to his table," Carl said.

"We cannot just go sit there; he'll suspect something", Leila said.

"Pretend you're checking out the table for a seat and when someone leaves, take their place," Carl offered.

"I will be across from you at the roulette table. If anything goes wrong, leave the table and don't wait for me," he continued.

Leila, without hesitation walked towards Bejar's table and stood there waiting for a seat to be vacated. Bejar glanced at her and immediately his face grew intent on hers. He gave her a quick smile, not saying anything. She played the game, reciprocating the same way. She calmly waited for few minutes until the guy sitting next to Bejar lost his money and decided he was done. She jumped in his seat. Bejar glanced at her again, this time the smile said, 'your money is mine and so are you' kind of attitude. After a couple of rounds, he decided it was time to strike up a conversation.

"It looks like your lucky night tonight," he commented.

"I guess," she replied.

"Can I offer you a drink?" he asked

"Thank you, but I'll pass this time," she said.

Accepting a drink from Bejar would have been risky, she thought. The safest rule was to decline an offer for a drink under the circumstances. From the roulette table Carl kept a close watch on both. He was getting a little anxious to know what was happening at their table. He wanted to approach the table thinking that perhaps he could overhear something but ultimately decided against it. He didn't want to jeopardize the mission.

Almost an hour later, over at the blackjack table, Leila stood up, picked up her chips and said, "that's it for me,"

Bejar wasn't going to just let her walk away. He stood up asking her if he could walk her out. She accepted. On their way out, Bejar's bodyguards started following and he stopped them. Leila nodded to Carl to follow. Carl made sure his gun was within reach under his coat. Leila and Bejar stepped out of the casino, walking toward her car with Carl following from a distance.

And once again Bejar asked if they could meet another time for a drink. He insisted and Leila said yes.

Chapter 14

THE RENDEZVOUS

The rendezvous was to take place at the Legacy Ottoman Hotel, located on Hamidiye Cd. No:16, 34112 Fatih/İstanbul. They met at around 9:30 pm. Leila picked the time because the hotel bar gets busy around 9:30 and if something had to happen, no one would notice because people will be too busy drinking and partying. Bejar was there first. He wasn't going to make the person he was attracted to wait, so he made sure that a table was waiting for her when she arrived. Leila showed up on time, which left Bejar beaming with joy that she didn't stand him up. He jumped out of his chair, greeting her and pulling her chair out. Carl, on the other hand, walked in and stood not too far from them. He faced Leila's direction, ready to jump in if needed. The waitress came by to take Leila's order since Bejar was already on his second drink.

"Hello," the waitress smiled, "what can I get for you?"

"A glass of your white wine," Leila said.

"Any preference for white?" The waitress needed clarification.

"What's a good Turkish white wine? Leila asked.

"We have a lot but the one most preferred by customers is the Kavaklidere Cankaya, however that comes only by the bottle, sorry."

"Anything else good by the glass?" Leila asked again.

"Sure, just bring the bottle of the Cankaya," Bejar interrupted the conversation.

But Leila insisted that she wanted only a glass. "Just a glass of your house white is fine," she indirectly ordered the waitress.

"And I'll have one more of these," Bejar said. It was a double shot of Amaretto with a twist of orange.

The waitress disappeared for a moment to get their order when Leila said, "Excuse me, I'll be right back" as she headed to the bathroom. She walked by Carl whispering "I am having wine and he's having Amaretto with a twist of orange."

The waitress was waiting for the order and she was chatting with a regular customer at the bar. The bartender set the drinks on the counter and moved on to other orders. At that time of night, it was several moments before the waitress picked up the drinks. In that time, Carl had already put something into Bejar's glass.

Leila was back at the table before the waitress brought the drinks. She made sure to return before her wine was on the table. Bejar started questioning Leila, curious to know who she was. "Are you from Turkey?"

"No, I am British," she answered. "And you?" she asked.

"I am from here." Bejar was being careful with his answers. "Are you visiting here or on business?" he asked.

"On business," she responded.

"What do you do?" he asked.

"I am in the jewelry business. I buy and sell custom made jewelry," she said. "And you?"

"I consult with businesses on their operations." He did not lie except that he avoided the details about his consulting services. Leila already knew what his consulting business was. She did not ask for details.

A few sips into his Amaretto and Bejar's speech started getting heavy. He tried to shake it off, but the stuff Carl slipped in his drink was too powerful for Bejar to fight. He started going back and forth out of consciousness when finally, his head fell flat on the table. A couple of people asked if he was okay, but Leila was quick to tell them he just had a little too much to drink.

Carl pretended to be one of the customers and rushed towards her asking, "Do you need any help?"

"Yes, please. I need to get him to the car," she replied.

Carl put Bejar's arm around his shoulder and headed toward the exit. They threw him into the car and drove off. The time was now almost 11:45 pm. They needed to get him to a secure place. The safe house was outside the city and that seemed the only logical place to take Bejar.

Early the next morning he woke up, not knowing what happened to him or how he ended up in this place. A few minutes later, Carl walked in.

"Who are you, and where am I?" Bejar asked.

"This is the United States of America government," Carl proudly replied.

"This is who?" Bejar felt confused and wanted to make sure he heard correctly.

Carl pulled up a chair and asked, "Where's Darkaoui"? Straight to the point.

"Who's Darkaoui?" Bejar replied.

"We're not going to play this game. You know who he is," Carl pressed. "No point in denying it; we have a video of you two together," he said.

"I have no idea who you're referring to," Bejar insisted.

Carl was frustrated by Bejar's responses. He got up, threw the chair out of the way and grabbed Bejar from the collar of his shirt.

As he started to threaten Bejar, Leila walked in. Bejar, upon seeing her while Carl's hands were on him said, "so what jewelry business are you in? The US spy business or the British one? I should've known that you were fake," he continued.

"You don't have any other options except to tell us everything about Darkaoui," she said. Bejar spat on the ground in a disgusted manner after Carl let go of him.

Leila and Carl left the room hoping that Bejar would come to his senses and give them the information about Darkaoui they wanted. But he wasn't about to do so. Carl made a quick phone call to Dani to find out if anything had happened in Malta or whether the weapons were picked up.

"Carl here," he said. "What the latest?"

"The shipment is on its way," Dani replied.

"You and Polina should take the first flight you can get find to Istanbul. We have much work to do here," Carl instructed Dani.

That same day, Dani and Polina boarded a plane from Malta to Turkey and the other two agents were dispatched to the CIA office in Italy. Istanbul, much like Spain, reminded Dani of his Arab roots; the buildings, the food, the people all brought him this nostalgic sentiment of his culture. He felt right at home.

Right away Carl, Dani, Leila and Polina got to work. Bejar now had four people to deal with. He would crack sooner or later and tell them what they wanted. Or so they thought. They tried everything they could with him - from intimidation to bribery and even starvation at times. There were no engagement rules to stick to at this point, any means necessary to make him talk were game, but as a former guerilla member, Bejar had a strong will to resist the most painful mental or physical maltreatment. He did it before when he was captured and tortured by the Iraqi military. He would exercise this mental seclusion that takes him out of reality to another world, known only to him, in which he could control his pain for hours. They kept him in the safe house guarded by the two CIA agents.

Darkaoui was on the loose and Bejar was making it difficult for Carl to find him. The Turkish secret service can certainly help, Carl told his team, but the problem is that the Turks will make a case against the Brits and the US governments for working solo without involving Turkey in an internal terrorism mission.

Dani proposed to Carl to have James deal directly with the Turkish government on this issue. Leila on the other hand suggested that the British government might be more successful than the US government, saying the US does not have a good reputation for playing the world's policeman. She explained to Carl that Turkey could be a real pain to deal with especially if they know the US secret service is meddling with their internal problems.

"I'd say that's not a good idea," she concluded.

Carl didn't care much about Leila or her unwanted sarcasm, but deep inside he accepted that she might have a point about the Turks being furious that other governments were getting involved in their affairs. Darkaoui was an internationally wanted man and he was up for grabs by any government, even the Turks, but telling the Turks how to do it- or what to do- was not going to fly with them.

Carl paused for a minute before telling his team "we're not involving anyone in this mission. Either we get the son of a b****ch out of Turkey alive to stand trial or we kill him here."

"I am not going to allow the Turks to jeopardize the mission," he continued in an upset voice. Dani, Polina, and Leila just listened. Dani, especially, knew Carl was serious about what he was saying; he knew him well. Carl looked at the three of them, saying, "if Bejar refuses to talk, we must find another way to get to the subject."

"What do you have in mind?" Leila questioned Carl.

"How did Bejar get to know the subject?" he asked.

"We need to find out who he talks to. Who are his connections- wherever they are," he said, "we need to find the names of other guerilla members operating in Turkey," Carl instructed. Infiltrating the guerilla group was not going to be an easy operation for Carl and his agents to do. They needed to move quickly if they wanted to find the subject. Carl thought another trip to the casino might lead them to someone close to Bejar. He and Dani he went back to the same luxurious casino. This time they remembered Mr. Demir, Omer (Carl), with the usual greeting of a tea at the entrance for both Carl and Dani. Dani bowed his head a little as a thank you before they were escorted inside. They stood for a few minutes together so as not to attract any attention, since security was everywhere. Then each went in a different direction, pretending to spend some money. Dani wasn't a gambler either. It is forbidden in the Muslim religion. He walked around some tables before sitting at the bar. Carl, on the other hand decided to play few rounds at the roulette table. Not before long, one of the two guys who were there before came in looking distressed. Carl never took his eyes from the door when he saw the guy come in. He quickly wrapped up his game again and left the table.

Joining Dani, he whispered, "he's one of the guys that, according to Leila, were talking about Bejar."

Dani looked at the guy briefly and turned his head back around. He didn't say anything. While Carl and Dani were keeping an eye on him, his phone rang.

"Slav" (hello in Kurdish), he answered the phone.

Carl and Dani could not understand what he was saying, but once again the name Bejar came up. This time it was loud and clear. That's all they needed to understand to make a connection.

The phone conversation didn't last long. The guy finished his drink, paid for it and left. Carl and Dani were behind him. They decided not to stop him but to follow him to wherever he was going.

A few blocks from the casino, he met with someone who didn't look very happy. Some yelling and cursing took place between the two while Carl and Dani kept a close watch. Although they could not hear what was going on, they were convinced that the argument had something to do with Bejar or even the subject Darkaoui. Carl decided to change the plan; he wasn't going to keep following these guys. The time was now to get some answers.

"Let's get to work," he said to Dani.

Chapter 15

THE FIGHT

In a sudden move, they jumped the two guys. Punches were exchanged. This was not a situation where you show secret service badges or try to play by any rules. The two guys were not easy to subdue; they pulled out their knives, waving them in Carl and Dani's faces. At one point, Dani's left arm was cut severely. He pulled out his belt and tried to use it as a weapon. When they tried to stab Dani again, Dani wrapped his belt around the guy's arm, moving it to one side, making him lose balance and fall to the ground. He dropped his knife and he tried to get up, but Dani punched him again as hard as he could, knocking him down. He retrieved his belt and wrapped it around the guy's neck. He held him down for few minutes. He wasn't breathing anymore. Carl on the other hand, did not waste any time. He pointed his gun right away at the second guy.

"Who does Bejar work for?" he yelled in his face. "I don't know anybody with that name," the guy said twice in broken English.

"You have one minute to make up your mind," Carl said in an intimidating tone.

"I don't know who he is," the guy insisted.

Carl was holding him down, reached in his pocket and pulled out a cell phone and his wallet. Dani walked up to Carl. His arm was wrapped with a piece of the dead guys shirt, and blood was seeping through from his wound.

Carl quickly glanced at him and said, "are you ok?" and returned his attention back to the guy.

He threw the wallet to Dani to check its contents. The name on his ID read 'Bebek Soran'. He was named after the village name where he was born. The wallet had also contained some money, some business cards and a piece of paper with an address and a phone number.

"Whose phone number and address are these?" Carl asked.

"I have never seen this paper before," Soran replied.

"It's in your wallet and you've never seen it?" Carl was still pointing the gun to Soran's head.

No response.

The phone contact list was long, and the texts were in Kurdish, which Carl and Dani could not read. But their break came when Carl found a message written in English to a foreign name.

The message read, "Bejar and the Egyptian are in contact." Right then, Carl knew that the Egyptian referred to was Darkaoui.

"Who was this message sent to?" he asked his prisoner.

"I don't know," Soran replied. Carl hit Soran in the face with the grip of his gun and now in pain, Soran realized that Carl was not joking.

"Who did you send the message to?" he asked him again.

"I don't know," he repeated, but then changed his mind when Carl pointed the gun between his eyes. "I swear, I don't know the name. I was given instructions to send the message to a phone number that was handed to me, that's all I know," Soran said.

"Send a text to this number," Carl ordered.

Trembling from the pain on his bruised face and from his fear of Carl, "what should I say?" he asked.

"I have some important information," Carl ordered him to write.

A few seconds later a reply came through.

"What information?" the receiver replied.

"He wants to know what the information is," Soran told Carl.

"Tell him you have someone who has information about Bejar and the Egyptian."

"Where are you?" the receiver asked.

"Not too far from the casino," Soran replied.

"Stay there!" was the response.

Carl told Soran who was still on the ground, "this is someone you know who told you that Bejar and the Egyptian are plotting to double cross the Kurdish Rebellion leader, so Bejar can become the new leader. This would allow the Egyptian to operate in both Turkey and Iraq."

A few minutes later, a car pulled up to the curb looking for Soran and the new guy. No one got out the car. Carl hid not too far away, while Soran and Dani headed toward the parked car. The window rolled down revealing a chubby face of a very heavy person. He looked at Soran and sized up Dani.

"What happened to your face?" he asked in a stern tone of voice.

"Nothing, just a fight outside the casino," Soran replied.

The heavy person was still looking at Dani with an uncomfortable facial expression. He told both of them to get in the car and ordered the driver to start moving.

Reliving the past, Dani was now on his way to a new operation infiltrating the Kurdish Rebellion. In reality, neither Carl nor Dani were interested in the Kurdish Rebellion. This was a Turkish and Kurdish problem. They figured they could use the Kurdish Rebellion as bait to get to the subject and his reformist group.

Carl understood that Dani would be in touch if something came up; he didn't need to tell him anything. The car sped up leaving town and after few kilometers, the driver got off the main road and steered towards a rugged mountainous terrain that was not too far off the main road. They came to a gate guarded by two guys with machine guns. Dani's first thought was that those guns were probably bought from the subject. He drew a mental picture of the surroundings and the two guards. This was the time for him to get acquainted with his new environment. The car stopped at the gate for a routine check before the driver waved them in. On the other side of the gate, the building that no one even suspected existed was like a fortress. The heavy guy got out first and was followed by the driver, then Soran and Dani. They walked inside when the heavy guy spoke.

"Wait here," he ordered Soran and Dani. He disappeared for a moment and came back. "Follow me," he ordered them again.

They made their way through a labyrinth of hallways before they found themselves standing in front of the Kurdish Rebellion leader, Berken Payan, an average height man with unusual facial complexities that revealed a fierce personality. His moustache extended from one side to the other, covering his entire mouth. He looked at Dani and Soran for a second, not saying anything, then taking few steps away. He turned around with his back to them and asked,

"How do you know Bejar?" He didn't mention the Egyptian.

"I worked for him," Dani replied.

"What kind of work?" Berken asked.

"I collected money for him from people who owed him and refused to pay him back," Dani said.

"What do you know about Bejar and the Egyptian? Berken asked.

"I once heard Bejar talking to an Egyptian guy about a change of role," Dani commented.

"What role?" Berken asked.

"I don't know," Dani replied.

That response didn't sit well with the Kurdish Rebellion leader. He turned around walked over to Dani, punching him in the stomach.

"That is not the response I want," he said in an angry voice.

"I am going to ask you again," he said. "What role were they talking about?" Berken asked again.

"They mentioned something indirectly like the rebellions and a need for new leadership," Dani replied.

"What's their plan?" Berken wanted more details.

"I don't know, they were very brief, that's all I heard," Dani said.

Berken was silent for few minutes then ordered to Soran, "Bring Bejar in, and find the Egyptian and get rid of him."

That was the timing Dani was waiting for.

"I can do that for you," he proposed to Berken.

Dani knew where Bejar was, but he was more interested in Darkaoui. "I can deal with the Egyptian. I have a personal score to settle with him," Dani offered.

Berken listened to Dani but wasn't sure if he should accept Dani's offer. "What score?" he asked.

"He set me up in a raw deal with some people who wanted me dead."

Berken continued listening, then said, "Soran, get me Bejar, and you find the Egyptian. Bring him to me alive, got it?" he insisted before walking away.

Dani had no idea where Darkaoui was but Soran might know, he thought. He had to quickly think of a way to get Soran to let him in on Darkaoui's whereabouts. Dani made a proposition to Soran he could not turn down. He told Soran that he could buy his freedom and live under an assumed name in any location he chose if he told him where Darkaoui was. At first, Soran refused because he didn't trust Dani. This is the guy that works for the government and there is no way he'll let me off the hook that easily, Soran thought to himself.

"Count me out of your plan," Soran told Dani. "I don't trust you. "Find the Egyptian yourself," he said.

"Listen, I am giving you a chance to save your skin from the federal US Federal prison system. You have no idea what that is like. You better think again," Dani tried to scare Soran.

"There's no way I will negotiate on your offer; I'll be dead before I can get anywhere," Soran explained.

"You'll be dead by Berken's command or jailed for life by the US government. If I were you, I would think seriously about the offer," Dani suggested.

Soran was now faced with making a decision that could either save him or see him killed. He agreed to Dani's offer with one condition. He wanted to be moved to the USA with a new identity.

"I can't promise that, Dani replied," but I'll see what I can do," he continued. "Now, where is the Egyptian?"

"I want something in writing," Soran pushed.

"I can't give you that. It's not up to me, I have to talk to the people in charge," Dani responded. "We have wasted enough time. Tell me where the Egyptian is," Dani was getting frustrated.

Soran, heaving a big sigh, looked up and down. "He's in a house outside of town," Soran finally said.

"Do you have an address?" Dani asked. Soran pulled out his phone, showing Dani the address to the house.

"Let's go!" Dani ordered Soran.

"You're on your own, I need to find Bejar", he said.

"You're coming with me; we'll deal with Bejar later," Dani ordered Soran.

"Why are you so interested in the Egyptian?" Soran was curious.

"None of your business," Dani said.

At nightfall they both headed out on the hunt for the Egyptian.

On the way Dani made a quick call to Carl. "I know where the subject is," and he texted him the address so they could meet at the location.

Carl didn't want to let Leila Al-Masi or even Polina know. This was his and Dani's mission. He jumped in a car and drove to the house.

Soran saw Carl and backed off. He remembered what happened to him with Carl.

Chapter 16

THE ARREST

Carl and Dani took their positions; Carl in the front and Dani watching the back. The lights were on. Carl peeked from the living room window and saw Darkaoui sitting at the dining room table texting. Dani had already entered the house from a back window. Darkaoui felt something unusual; his years of spying alerted him. He grabbed his gun and turned the lights off. He hid in a corner and waited. Carl picked the lock and opened the door quietly. Soran followed him inside. Carl brought Soran in, so he wouldn't take off if Carl left him outside. Darkaoui remained hiding, waiting with his gun pointed at the front door. In the dark, it was difficult to see who was where or who was who. He fired the first shot, Carl fired back, Dani kept silent. His plan was to capture Darkaoui alive. Carl fired again. This time Darkaoui's shot went straight at Soran, killing him on the spot. Dani saw where Darkaoui's shots were coming from. He shot Darkaoui, hitting him in the chest; he fell with blood gushing from his left side. Carl and Dani rushed to him because they wanted him alive. They put him in the car and rushed him to the closest hospital in town. While the emergency staff took him in, the front desk nurse asked for his information.

"What's his name?" she asked.

"Baker Joseph," Carl quickly made up a name.

"How was he hit?" she asked.

"He got mugged and when he tried to run, they shot him."

"Do you know him?" she kept asking.

"Yes, he works for me," Carl announced.

"Can I get and address and a phone number?" she asked.

"Sure," said Carl giving the address of the house where Darkaoui was hiding as well as Soran's phone number.

Darkaoui was in surgery for a few hours before being wheeled to a room. Still unconscious, both Carl and Dani stood in his room waiting for him to wake up.

"Visiting hours are over, please leave now," the night nurse said.

Carl and Dani were not about to leave Darkaoui alone. They knew that would be a costly mistake. After a short argument with the head nurse they convinced her that they would wait in the waiting room. She agreed. Around 3:30 in the morning, the hospital was totally quiet. Carl decided to take a walk in the hallway to check things out. Nothing unusual, however, something caught his attention: a male nurse pushing a food cart towards Darkaoui's room. Carl was curious why a nurse would bring food to Darkaoui at 3:30 am? He was still unconscious from his surgery. He rushed to the room to find the nurse trying to suffocate Darkaoui with a pillow. He wrestled him to the ground at which point nurses and security rushed to the room, but whoever was trying to get rid of Darkaoui was able to free himself from Carl and run before hospital security got to him.

"We have the subject and we need to secure him. He's in the hospital. We shot him in a standoff," Carl told James. "But we have another problem," he continued.

"What now?" James responded in an unpleasant tone.

"Someone tried to get to him at the hospital", Carl explained.

"Listen, keep the bastard alive. Whatever you have to do. I don't care if he dies, but not now. We need him to get to whoever is behind him," James insisted.

"I don't think the safe house is a good idea; I think the Embassy is a better bet to keep him secure for now," Carl suggested.

"I'll call there and speak to the head of secret service," James offered. "'ll be in touch," he said and ended the call.

This time it was Carl and Dani's turn to kidnap Darkaoui from the hospital. After 24 hours they decided it was time to get him out before someone else tried again to get to him. However, they could not just check him out. The only way was to sneak him out. While Carl stood guard in front of the room, Dani threw on a nurse's gown, got Darkaoui dressed, stuck him in a wheelchair and wheeled him out. Carl rushed outside to bring the car closer to the front of the hospital, but the night security guard had his doubts about someone being checked out that late at night. He stopped Dani at the exit.

"Gentlemen, I need to see the patient discharge papers," he ordered.

"He's not checking out, I am just taking him out for some air," Dani replied. The guard looked at Dani and Darkaoui for few seconds and said. "Ok, right outside the door."

They stepped outside, waited until the guard got distracted with a phone call and Dani sped up to the car. By the time the guard realized something was wrong, they were already gone. He called security who ran all over the hospital and all over the parking lot, but it was too late.

James had already set up a hiding place for the subject in the US Embassy. The head of the secret service was waiting for Carl and Dani to pull up in their car. The Embassy security waved the car in, led by the head of the secret service. Still a little bit sedated, Darkaoui had his eyes wide open but did not seem to know what was going on - or so he pretended. Now underground in the huge compound, they led him to a room at the end of a long hallway where they locked him in. In the middle of the night two agents showed up to the room, sat him down and started questioning him. Darkaoui was just staring at them.

The interrogation began.

"Who do you work for?" the agents asked.

"I don't know," Darkaoui responded.

"Who do you report to?" the agents persisted.

"I don't know," Darkaoui kept saying, pretending to be out of it.

"You know there's no out from here," one agent said.

"You can either cooperate or you will die here; no one will get to you here," the second agent commented. "So, if I were you, I would come clean and maybe, just maybe, you'll get a deal."

Darkaoui, upon hearing the word 'deal' thought twice about it but he wasn't going to jump on that yet. He wanted more. He wanted to be acquitted entirely from any charges and freed. He knew how to play the bargain game.

"What kind of deal are we talking about?" he wanted to know.

"It depends on your cooperation," the agent replied.

"That's not good enough for me. I need a signed promissory note that all charges will be dropped," Darkaoui said, playing hard to get.

"Can't do that. It is not up to you to decide. Consider yourself lucky that we are even talking to you," the senior agent said with a voice full of rage.

"Now, who do you report to?" the agent asked again.

Darkaoui, silent with his hands cuffed, did not answer. "I want a lawyer", was the only thing he said.

"Come again?" the agent said, followed by a laugh.

"You're f*****g kidding me! A lawyer for what?" he asked. "No lawyer on this planet is going to talk to you, let alone take your case," the agent continued. "You know what, we're done here. You will be shipped to the US in the next 24 hours to stand trial there and guess what, no lawyer will help you. Sons of b***ches like you have changed how the legal system works. You'll either rot in jail the rest of your life or you will be executed, that I can guarantee you," and the agents walked out of the room.

The agents' threats made Darkaoui understand that this was no game. He has no other choice but to talk. He asked the guard outside his door to see the agents.

They walked in and said, "you asked to see us?"

"Let's talk about my safety first," Darkaoui started the conversation. "I need to know that you will guarantee my safety if I tell you what you want to know," he continued.

"We'll get to that later," one of the agents replied.

"You tell us everything you know, and we'll try to help you," the senior agent said.

"Ok, how do you want to do this?" Darkaoui asked.

"We'll record your statement," the second agent said.

The senior agent nodded to his partner who disappeared for a few minutes and returned with a laptop. They set it up, turned the camera on and started the questioning. "Your full name," the senior agent asked.

"Naim Darkaoui," he replied.

"Your origin?" the questioning continued.

"I am Egyptian," the subject replied.

"Your profession," the agent asked.

Darkaoui paused for a second, trying to think of what a good answer would be.

"Your profession?" the agent asked again.

"An international weapons dealer," Darkaoui replied.

"Who do you buy and sell your weapons to?" the agent asked.

"I buy them from different countries and sell them to freedom fighter groups," he said.

"You mean to terrorists," the agent interrupted him.

"Call them whatever you want. I provide them what they need, and I do not ask what they do with the weapons. I am in it for the money," Darkaoui argued.

The senior agent asked his partner, stop the recording and turned around to Darkaoui, "Stop the BS, you're not in it just for the money. You killed people and you formed the Reformists group; that's not just for the money," the senior agent said sounding mad.

Darkaoui smiled, shaking his head.

"It was not my desire to form the reformists; I was ordered to lead the group."

The recorder was back on.

"What do you know about the Reformist group?" the senior agent asked. "Who are they, and what's their motive?"

"I founded the group under the orders of some powerful people who had a vested interest in creating the reformists," Darkaoui explained.

"Who are these people?" the agent asked.

"I don't know who they are, all I know is that they always gave orders through somebody else," he said.

"Who is this person?"

"I never met him; it's always been by phone," he said

"Do you have his contact info?"

"No, I never called him, he always called me. "

"The weapons in the warehouse in Malta, who were they supposed to go to?"

"To the Reformists and the Kurdish Rebellion group."

"Who was in contact with you about the weapons?"

"The same guy who called me every time."

"How do you know the Kurdish rebellion leader?"

"I was introduced to him by someone name Bejar."

"For what reason?"

"He needed weapons for his Kurdish fighters in Iraq."

"Did you provide him with the weapons?"

"No, we were still negotiating a deal."

"Who is this Bejar?"

"I believe he's the Kurdish rebellion leader's top Lieutenant."

"About the Reformist group, who's behind them?"

"I don't know," Darkaoui said, showing a little frustration.

"Give me some names. I am sure you must have some idea who is behind the group", the senior agent insisted.

"Kabil Chanaf, The director of the Hedge Fund (Stoneridge Associates), Moussi Fenak, a general of the armed forces, Abad Assad, CEO of the Blue Water investment company, and two others high-ranking foreigners. I don't know who they are." Darkaoui said.

"Did you have a direct contact with these individuals?"

"No, I never met them, but I know about them from my sources," Darkaoui said.

"What's their agenda?"

"These are people who know how the system works and they are after political positions, forming allies and putting them in charge in other countries so they can control the vast majority of the wealth in those countries. Your administration is aware of that, but they chose not to do anything about it so long as your country's interest are protected in those places. The people behind the Reformists will safeguard your country's interest in oil and other natural resources, and in exchange, your government will guarantee safety and political power to Chanaf, Fenak, and Assad. It's an economic game, no more or less and you know that." Darkaoui said.

The questioning lasted close to three hours with Darkaoui providing the agents all the information they needed.

Carl and Dani went back to meet with Polina at the safe house. Leila Al-Masi was nowhere to be found. Carl figured she must be somewhere in Istanbul looking for Darkaoui. She didn't know he was already in US custody. Carl and Dani were not about to blow the mission by letting Leila in on the plan. There was little trust between the US government and the British government because of the tension that built up between them from before.

At the safe house, Carl and Dani found Polina and one agent dead, the other agent was barely alive, and Bejar gone.

"Who did this?" Dani asked the agent.

"Four guys stormed in and started shooting. One of them is dead over there."

The agent was barely able to speak.

"Did they say anything?" Carl asked.

"No, they just started shooting, took the prisoner and left."

He was breathing hard.

Dani walked toward the dead person and pulled back his face cover.

"He looks like one of Bejar's guerillas," he told Carl.

By the time they got the information from the wounded agent, he was dead.

Carl and Dani destroyed everything in the safe house, packed up all the documents even taking Polina's and the agents' badges, guns and other stuff. Dani made an anonymous call to the police to report the murders and they both left the house. The Turkish police could not find anything to solve the murder case. The investigation determined that this was a robbery gone wrong.

Bejar was not much of a concern now since Darkaoui was in custody. The secret service had enough information to build their case. They will let the Turkish government take over trying to find Bejar and deal with the Kurdish rebellion leader at the right time.

Even though Darkaoui had given the US government enough information to go after the top leaders of the Reformist group, the US government could not arrest them since this was outside the US government jurisdiction. However, the information the US had now was a gold mine for the US government to use to further its interest in those countries. Playing the bad cop and the good cop was something that the Administration was not going to let pass. The plan now was clear. Although the US cannot pursue Chanaf, Fenak, and Assad or the other three foreigners, they could leverage the information they had to secure a stronger presence in Gulf region

A few days later a meeting was set between the US top Diplomat, the Secretary of State and the leaders of some Gulf countries to discuss a deal. The round of trips started in Iraq, where the Secretary of State met with government leaders and laid the foundation for the new US's plan. Vincent Waters was a veteran diplomat with an extensive career in politics as a negotiator. He was known as the 'Tactician'. There was no deal he would fail to close. He started his negotiations with a friendly speech.

"It's always a great pleasure to visit friends," he would say. "The US appreciates your friendship and cooperation very much," he continued. "I am here because we have credible information that some groups are planning to cause harm to your country and overthrow your government," he explained.

The same speech was related to each leader of those countries and the same question was asked by each of those leaders.

"Who are these groups?"

"The two groups are the Reformists and the Kurdish Rebellion groups. Since we cannot arrest or put these groups on trial in the US as you know, the US government has the duty to alert you of the danger your countries face," Waters said.

"Have these groups been located, and do you know their names?" The leaders wanted to know.

"We have the names of their leaders and in fact, we have one of the leading members in custody right now," Waters announced.

"What's the US government's interest in sharing this information with us?" The Iraqi Prime Minister asked.

"In addition to protecting the US interest in Iraq, we want to make sure that the country is not destabilized. Your government has done a lot of work to bring stability to the region and we want it to stay that way," Waters hinting at something more.

"What's your Administration's plan?" The Prime Minister asked.

"We can help you stop any threat from the Reformist and the Kurdish Rebellion group," Waters got straight to the point.

Interrupting in mid-sentence, the Prime Minister asked, "What are you proposing in exchange?"

"The only way we can prevent these groups form taking action is for your government to allow the US to have more presence here by bringing in more boots to secure your oil wells," Waters said.

"We're not turning the country into another US State," the Prime Minister replied. "You already have your soldiers here, in fact, your Administration should start thinking about planning to withdraw your soldiers from the country as soon as possible."

The Prime Minister was now getting annoyed by Waters' proposition.

"This is a sovereign country and your work here is done. The groups you're referring to - we'll deal with them on our own terms," the Prime Minister continued.

"I think you are making a mistake sir. This is big and from the intelligence we have gathered, these groups are very powerful. They have followers in more than one country. They can hit anywhere at any time," Waters insisted.

"Let's be honest, Mr. Secretary, your Administration is more worried about your country's interest than what could happen to my country, we both know that. Your visit is not out of concern for my country's stability but to convince us that without your help we can't deal with the problem ourselves. And you and I know that. Today you're asking us to allow in more boots and tomorrow you will put more conditions in exchange for your help." The Prime Minister was pushing back. " Further, I understand that you have the right to not share with the us the list of the so called groups your Administration has, but let's be clear, not only my government but every government in the region will hold your government responsible if these groups carry out their plans to destabilize any part of the Middle East." The Prime Minister warned.

"This sounds like a threat, Mr. Prime Minister," Waters said with a forced smile.

"It's not a threat my friend, it's just setting an understanding for the future," the Prime Minister replied.

The meeting was over. Waters was on his way to other neighboring countries. He got the same cold shoulder in every country in the region he visited. The message from the leaders in the region was clear; we are not going to let the US Administration dictate the rules.

Vincent Waters was mad as hell and called the CIA Director telling him, "Screw them, let them deal with their own f******g problems. They can go after their own people, we're done," he fumed.

Waters wasn't mad because he couldn't get the leaders to agree with his offer, he was mad because he couldn't secure more interests for the US in the region. Arab countries were now held hostage because Washington was not sharing the information, they needed to face the Reformists and the Kurdish Rebellion group, and Waters did not have a problem with that. He wanted them to accept his deal. Upon his arrival to the White House he met with the President and the Vice President to debrief them.

"So, what's your plan since they didn't agree with your offer?" The Vice President asked.

"That was a waste of time," Waters replied. "They were not interested in cooperating," he continued. "You two figure a way around this to get them to accept the deal."

"Maybe we should talk to some of our friends in Europe; they may help us get through to these leaders," the Vice President proposed.

"You two take care of this. I don't want the Europeans to get involved in the region if the intelligence we have on these secret cells - the Reformists and the Kurdish Rebellions - leaks out. That will put the Europeans in a bargaining position for their help. This situation needs to be dealt with immediately," the President ordered the Vice President and the Secretary of State.

Jonathan and Vincent walked out of the president's office trying to come up with a plan.

"I'll make some phone calls," the Vice President said.

"Let me know what you find out and I will think of something too," Waters replied.

A few seconds later, Waters' phone rang. "Walters here," he answered.

"It's me," the Vice President said. "Can you get me the list of countries in the region we give aid to?" he asked.

"Sure, I'll get to it right away," Waters replied.

The next morning the list of countries was on the VP's desk. That was the first order of business on Tuesday morning

The VP got on the phone immediately, calling some of his counterparts in the Middle East. He would start the conversation with Assalam Alaikum in broken Arabic, followed by a laugh from both sides of the phone.

"This is the vice president of the United States of America, Jonathan Evans. How are you?"

"Fine, Mr. VP, and you?"

"Very good, thank you," he replied.

The small talk did not last long. Jonathan was on a mission and the president was waiting for answers.

"Listen", he said, "I am calling to talk to you about the aid your country gets every year from my Administration. I am afraid that we have to reduce it for an undetermined period moving forward."

"Is there an issue we're not aware of for making this decision"? The Egyptian counterpart asked.

"Well, as you know the global economy is not doing very well because of the political uncertainty and all of terrorism happening in the world, and we believe it's better if we cut down on our aid to some countries," Jonathan explained. "The issue with oil prices and the unstable global economy are not helping. We tried to make a deal with some of the leaders in your part of the world, but they wouldn't cooperate, so we decided to slow things down."

"What deal, if I may ask?" the Egyptian VP inquired.

"Well, so long as the threat of terrorism is out there, we are all faced with it. We need to work together to bring stability not only to your region, but to the world. Some of the Arab leaders are refusing to let the US help weed out these terrorist groups in their country," Jonathan was selling the plan.

"Of course, we need to do something about it, and my government is willing to help in any way possible," the

Egyptian VP said, knowing he needed to secure the financial aid his country gets from the US.

"I need you to try to convince some of those leaders to consider our offer to help," Jonathan announced. If you can make arrangements with them to do so, that will be great and my administration would really appreciate that," he continued.

"Let me talk to them and see what happens," the Egyptian VP said.

A few days later, a meeting between Vincent Waters and some of the Arab countries leaders was set in Cairo. The agreement to meet in Cairo was purposely intended by the Egyptian government as a message to the US Administration that 'we took care of business and that aid better keep coming.'

After hand shaking and greetings, a closed-door meeting took place for two days with Waters and his team negotiating with the Arab leaders. There were some promising results but not as much as the US was hoping to get out of the it.

"Our plan is clear" one of leaders said. "We give you a year to help us stabilize the region from any terrorist threats, but certainly no military bases and no more US boots in the region," he continued.

"I understand, however, you must also understand that without extra boots on the ground we will not be able to control the situation if something happens," Waters said.

"That's your assumption, sir," said Zulaif Kamssi, head of the Arab Coalition Against Terrorism.

"What we need from your Administration are the tools and the necessary intelligence to deal with the terrorism problem, but no boots. We have enough of your soldiers here already," he continued.

Waters tried to interrupt him, but Zulaif had to finish what he had to say. Waters just listened.

"Our conditions are clear," Badr Humais, said a top General and Director of the Arab International Task Force.

The AITF was founded after the dark years of terrorism that hit North Africa and some of the Gulf countries extremely hard. The governments in those countries agreed to put together a task force for cooperation on military intelligence. All members of that force were top military officers and top-secret service agents with only one career all their lives: a military one. So they knew very well what was at stake, and understood that allowing the US to bring any show of force to the region would only make the terrorism situation worse.

"Now, we are aware that you have information about certain groups who are active in our countries. Your Administration has the responsibility to share that information with us. This activity is happening beyond your country's border and we will take care of our internal affairs ourselves," Humais said to Waters.

"As I mentioned to you all during my previous trip to the region, we do have some information, and we are still trying to confirm the validity of that intelligence," Waters said, playing the political game.

Waters wasn't happy with the deal he got. He was not willing to share the information unless the deal changed in his favor.

"We'll have to go back and assess the accuracy of the intelligence we have before we can give you a full report on these groups or names," he continued.

His Director of Intelligence, Michael Wall, looked at him knowing that Waters was not telling the truth, but he could not contradict him. He kept quiet.

During dinner, Waters pulled aside the Egyptian VP, thanking him for setting up the meeting and to express his disagreements with the conditions put on the table.

"They could've done better than those conditions. We are not going to waste our time for a whole year and then leave if something happens. We might have to do it all over again. The deal they proposed is not in the United States' interest," he said.

"They are not going to change their position", the Egyptian VP replied. "I had conversations with all of them before you arrived and they made it clear that they don't want any US military involved in their states' affairs," he commented.

After dinner Waters went back to his hotel and called Jonathan, giving him the details of the meeting. "He's not going to like this," Jonathan said to Waters about the President's reaction.

"Where did you leave it with them?" Jonathan asked

"We ended the meeting with their offer on the table for now. But I am thinking it's not over yet."

"I hope not," Jonathan said, thinking there would be further discussions before reaching another agreement, but Waters was not totally clear on what he meant by 'it's not over yet.' Their phone conversation ended with that.

The next morning, Jonathan shared with the President what Waters reported. He also made sure to relate to him that Arab leaders made it clear that if something happened in their countries, they would hold the US Administration responsible for withholding important intelligence information about terrorist groups operating in their countries.

The President was silent for a minute then told Jonathan, "Give them the information and tell Waters to back off. We'll find other ways to protect our interests in the region."

With this intelligence now in their possession, Badr Humais and the other military officials from the rest of the countries began the process of eliminating the Reformists and the Kurdish Rebellion groups, but mostly after Chanaf, Fenak, and Assad. In the meantime, Darkaoui was extradited to Egypt where he would stand trial for arms trafficking and for his involvement with the Reformist group. He was escorted by the Turkish government in a private jet chartered by the US government so as not to raise any suspicions that traveling commercial would bring. Arriving to Cairo airport in chains, Darkaoui seemed happy to be back in Egypt, even though was heading straight to prison. He looked around, hearing people speaking his native language. The familiar scents of Egypt made him feel good. He was handed over by the US secret service to Egyptian authorities and they threw him in an armored car followed by an unmarked car and sped away. Darkaoui might have been feeling better that he was no long in US custody, but he was no better off being in the custody of the Egyptians. Egyptian jail was no walk in the park unless you could buy off some dirty guards looking to make extra cash. For months, Darkaoui sat in jail with no trial date set.

Only after his lawyer pushed hard was a date set for him; he would begin his trial on June 10th. The courtroom was not open to the public; just the judge, the defense, and the prosecution were present in the court room. This was an extremely sensitive case of homeland security for Egypt and the classified details, including names were about to be presented needed not to be leaked out

On June 10th, the day of Darkaoui's trial, the area outside the court was packed with people waiting to see this notorious terrorist, as he was described by the media, brought to the court room. Security was heavy and police cars blocked the entire street waiting for the prison van to pull up to the courthouse. But the van never showed up and the trial never took place. Later that day, the news media announced that Darkaoui was found dead in his cell from an apparent suicide.

From the information obtained from the US Secret Service, the Egyptians started the hunt for the Reformists and their leaders both inside Egypt and outside with the raid extending to other countries in the region. Several members of the Reformist group were arrested, and others killed, but

Chanaf, Fenak, and Assad were nowhere to be found. Apparently, news of Darkaoui's testimony somehow found its way to the three of them. The three foreign names on the list were never found.

With Darkaoui and the Reformists out of the way now, Carl and Dani were still faced with dealing with a dangerous group. The Kurdish guerillas had to be stopped from any terrorist operations in Iraq and Turkey because the guerillas' leader was not only interested in changing the governing system in Iraq, but Turkey was another country the Rebellion group had on its terrorist operations agenda. But James Foster wasn't on board with Carl. He told him to let the Turks deals with the guerillas.

"Our mission is done, "James told Carl. "We should just hand the information about this Rebellion group to the Turkish authorities and let them solve their own problems." Although Carl didn't totally agree, he had no choice but to comply.

A couple of days later Carl had a meeting set up with the Chief of the Turkish Secret Service (MIT) to share the information with him but was surprised to learn that the Turkish government was ahead of the game. The Turks already knew about the rebellion guerrillas and their moves. Apparently Soran and another person were not just members of the rebellion group but were also informants for the Turkish government. The Chief of the Secret Service even knew about Carl and Dani's presence in Turkey.

"We want you to leave Turkey in the next twenty-four hours" the chief told Carl. "Your business is done here. The only reason we didn't come after you is because we were instructed not to," the chief continued." We were informed that your friend met with the Rebellion leader and we knew about the Egyptian and Bejar."

"Why did your government wait to go after them?" Carl wanted to know.

"We have our own way of doing things. It's not the Americans or anyone else who's going to tell us how to operate", the chief replied, seeming annoyed by Carl's question.

"But you realize that this group is not just a threat to your country's security but also to other places in the Gulf," Carl said.

"You mean where American interests are, "the chief quickly said.

"Well, that's true," Carl replied.

"What your government decides to do outside Turkey is its own business, but here our interests come first, and your government has no business interfering in Turkey's internal affairs," the chief said. "I suggest that your government leave Turkey to the Turks. We know how to handle our own problems," the chief admonished.

The meeting ended with a pleasant exchange and yet, was a little tense as Carl and the chief of MIT played by different rules. With Polina's death and Leila Al-Masi being out of the picture - probably on another mission or back to Britain - the Brits were informed by James's boss that Darkaoui's case was out of their hands and that the US was no longer interested in pursuing it. The US government never told the Brits that the US worked out a deal with the leaders of the Arab region and Darkaoui was arrested in Turkey and extradited to Egypt. The American's interests had to be protected.

Chapter 17

THE RECKONING

Carl and Dani were not yet ready to leave Turkey despite the Chief of MIT's order to Carl to 'get out of the country in twenty-four hours.' They were now tasked with gathering intelligence about the guerillas and other terrorist groups operating in Turkey. These groups were part of an international terrorist network. After a series of terrorist attacks, Turkey became a hotspot and the US government intervention was necessary.

Although James Foster told Carl to back off the Rebellion group case, he mentioned to Carl that the work in Turkey was not done yet.

"We need to know which groups are active there," James said. "We know that the Kurdish rebels are planning attacks but what we need to know is who else is involved. The situation from Iraq to Syria is not just a Kurds involvement; other groups are also in the game according to the intelligence we have," James continued. "This is another delicate operation and you know the drill," James told Carl.

After Carl shared James' message with Dani, they set out to execute the plan. One advantage they had was that Dani had already made a connection in Turkey that might be useful. During their time in Turkey, Dani was frequently going to this little place where he enjoyed a nice Turkish kebab. He developed a relationship with the server and they often had a conversation. The server felt comfortable with Dani once he knew Dani had Arab origins. They would talk about life in Turkey; the people, the lifestyle, and he culture. A few weeks went by and the friendship between them was getting closer. Sometimes they would meet on the server's days off for coffee or lunch. As conversations between the two became more open, the server, Akam Aslan, would bring up discussions about politics and religion. Dani was still unsure if he should take part in those conversations, so he would only ask Akam his opinions. "I am not the person with all the answers," Akam said. "Everything that is happening in the world is just so confusing," he commented.

"How so?" Dani asked.

"You see some living a good life and they take advantage of their status in societies and others more educated are suffering. Take my situation. I have been to college and yet, the only job I can find is serving Kebab in a restaurant. It's very frustrating." he added.

"Your government does not provide you with any jobs or help when you finish college?" Dani pushed.

"No, we're left on our own," Akam replied. "My oldest brother is in the same situation; he graduated five years ago as an engineer and still can't find a job. Next time we meet I'll invite him to join us," Akam announced.

"I look forward to meeting him," Dany replied. The following week Dani, Akam and his brother met at a café shop not too far from Akam's work.

"Hello, this is my brother, Agryn."

"Hello sir, please call me Dani, short for Madiane," Dani replied.

"What's the origin of the name?" Agryn asked. "I have a lot of Arab friends and I have never heard that name before."

"It's a common Arabic name used in many parts of Arab countries, actually."

"Ah, I see. Interesting."

"What you are doing in Turkey?" Agryn was curious, speaking in broken English. Dani spoke Arabic, French, Spanish, and English but although Agryn spoke Arabic, Dani spoke to him in English so Agryn's brother could understand them since he didn't know Arabic

"I come here often for business" Dani replied. "Akam told me you're an engineer?"

"Yes," Agryn briefly replied.

"What type engineering do you specialize in?"

"I am sorry, can you repeat, I didn't understand," Agryn said. Akam repeats in Kurdish, "he asked you what your engineering specialty is."

"Oh, oh," he laughed, "Chemical Engineering."

"Akam told me you're out of work, that's unfortunate," Dani said, fishing.

"Yes, five years wasted in college and no future," Agryn replied.

"So, what do you do, now?" Dani was curious.

"Not much. I sometimes do a side project if someone needs engineering advice. I also do repair work to make some money," Agryn replied.

"I also went to engineering school back home, but it was electrical engineering for me. I have always been interested in electrical work," Dani lied.

"Really? You should talk to my two friends, Alaz and Amanc. They are also electrical engineers," Agryn offered.

He then turned to his brother and said in Kurdish, "bring him to dinner at the house on the weekend. He can meet them there."

"What is he saying?" Dani asked. "He's inviting you to dinner at his place to meet his friends, "Akam translated.

"Sure, thank you!" Dani replied

On Saturday evening Dani and Akam met at the usual café, and then headed to Agry's place in the city. Agry's apartment was a small one bedroom flat tucked at the end of an old building resembling Ottoman era architecture. They were greeted by Agryn opening the door.

"Come in," he offered with a smile.

They removed their shoes in the small hallway and proceeded to the living room which was arranged in a Turkish Style décor featuring Arabic style called 'majlis' which translates to 'sitting'. Four long benches lined up in an "L" shape covered with expensive upholstery with matching pillows used as kuchens and others as arm rests on each bench, and a hand-woven rug covered the mosaic tile floor. Decorations on the walls revealed the Turkish and Kurdish history throughout time. Photos of Kurdish leaders hang on the wall. Two other guys were already there; introductions took place and Dani started immediately scanning the environment. He noticed a photo of Agryn posing in a picture with another person holding a rifle.

"Is that you in the picture?" he asked Agryn.

"Yes," Agryn said before turning to his brother to translate. "Tell him this was on a hunting trip."

The other two guests seemed a little uncomfortable not knowing who Dani was and their conversation was limited to short sentences. Dinner and tea were served a few minutes later. While enjoying the Turkish feast, Almanc's phone rang.

"Merheba," (hello in Kurdish) he answers.

He excused himself; taking the call, he walked toward the window a few feet away.

"Sorry," he said when he returned few minutes later.

He then turned to his friend Alaz and started speaking in Kurdish. Dani could not understand what the conversation was about but could tell that something was wrong.

Then Almanc stood up and said, "I have to leave. Something important came up and I have to go now," he announced.

Dani, Agryn, Akam, and the other Alaz continued talking while having tea.

"I don't understand, you guys seem to be so smart from what I see, and you can't find a job," Dani commented.

"It's the corruption here that is preventing us from finding jobs," Akam proposed.

"I know exactly how you must feel. I had the same problem back home when I graduated. I looked for a job for months and found nothing if I didn't pay someone or know someone," Dani said. "At least you guys can do a side job and get paid for it, I didn't have that chance."

"We don't like the jobs we do but we are forced to do it and we do it for money only," Alaz offered.

Agryn looked at Alaz to stop him from talking, but Alaz ignored him.

"Why forced?" Dani asked.

"We are ordered to put parts together and we have no idea what they are used for."

"We make them, get paid little money and nothing more. We have so much work and they don't want to hire some other people," Alaz said.

"Maybe I can help you if you have extra work."

"That would be great" Alaz replied, but Agryn didn't look enthusiastic about the idea.

"He's an electrical engineer. We do our part and he does what's needed," Alaz suggested to Agryn. "What do you think – should we talk to Almanc?" Alaz asked Agryn.

"I am not sure if he'll agree, but you can try."

"We don't know this guy," Almanc later told Alaz.

"We need someone with experience in electrical work," Alaz told Almanc.

Almanc reluctantly agreed to bring Dani in but not without trying to find out who Dani was. "You need to find out everything you can about him before he can be in."

No information was ever found about Dani. The papers he had were all fake. His fake passport provided by James said, 'Jordanian born' and literally every detail about him was not true. In a way it bothered Dani that he had no real identity, but this was his new life and he had come to terms with that. Dani was now part of the group that Almanc was using to create disturbances in Turkey and beyond. As days went by, Dani started discovering things that convinced him that these terrorists groups had a heavy agenda. Their operations were well planned, and they knew exactly where their targets were. Almanc was the mastermind, making every decision about operations where they were to take place, when and how. Agryn and Akam did not entirely agree with him on certain decisions but they could not go above him. He was one of the guerillas, much like Bejar. He didn't give people a second chance. Even though Dani and Almanc spent lots of time together now that Dani had become a member of the guerillas, he and Almanc did not feel comfortable around each other. Almanc kept his distance from Dani and so did Dani, in the beginning at least.

On one of the nights Almanc was getting ready to head out to meet with some of his soldiers to finalize the details of an operation. There was a plan to attack a Turkish financial district. Although Dani did not know about Almanc's plans, he knew that Almanc was planning something. He followed him from a distance to find out where he was going and who he was meeting with. Almanc disappeared in a dark alley that was barely noticeable from the street and Dani wondered if he should keep following him. He thought maybe Almanc knew someone was following him and he was waiting for him. Dani hesitated for a minute then decided to keep following Almanc. Not too far in the alley, Dani saw Almanc going into apartment number 25G. He waited and a few minutes later saw Almanc and two other guys leaving the apartment carrying bags.

He didn't follow them, instead he decided to check the inside of the apartment. Picking the lock was not an easy job for Dani; he fought with the tightly secured lock for almost 10 minutes before he could open it. The apartment was totally empty except for some chairs scattered around, a couple of tables and a large inventory of computers, wires, phones devices, and transmitters. Dani very quickly understood that this was the nerve center for Almanc and his terrorist group's planned operations. He took some photos of the stuff in the apartment and texted them to Carl.

Carl and Dani met to decide on a plan of action now that they had some photos as evidence but going after Almanc directly would be difficult because the computers, phones and transmitters were not enough to build a case against him. They needed more than that. The only way they could really know what Almanc was up to was to turn Akam and his brother Agryn. Dani's idea was to get to Akam initially and let him work on his brother. Carl didn't have a problem with Dani's plan.

A couple of days later Dani met with Akam at the usual café shop. At first, he was not sure how to approach the plan, but when Akam said during the conversation. "I am worried about my brother. He's been spending too much time with Almanc and I've never trusted that guy very much." Dani jumped on the opportunity to try and convince Akam to work with him.

"Honestly, I don't trust that guy either. I think he's up to something and someone needs to stop him. Has he ever mentioned to you or to your brother anything about his plans?" Dani asked.

"No, never, he's very secretive about everything he does and the people he deals with," Akam replied. "He hires me and Agryn when he needs us then he disappears for weeks before we see him again."

"Where does he go for weeks?" Dani wondered.

"I am not sure, when we ask him, he says 'visiting family'," Akam said. "I think he lies because his family is all here. They fled Iraq when the Iraqi government started clamping down on Kurdish people. We all fled," Akam explained.

"Are you all Kurdish?" Dani acted surprised.

"Yes, but the Turks don't know that, otherwise they would either jail us or kill us," Akam said.

"I think we need to do something to stop Almanc from going through with whatever plan he has. I don't want him to use my expertise in electrical engineering if he's planning to use it for something bad," Dani said. "And I think he's doing the same thing with you, your brother and all the others who work for him," he continued.

Almanc was not dumb and he was always suspicious of everyone he came in contact with, even those who he knew for a long time. Akam and Agryn were no exception; that is why he had eyes on them.

Later in the week he pulled Agryn aside and told him, "You need to tell your brother to keep his distance from the new recruit."

Agryn told him he would. Although Agryn reported to Almanc, he did not see eye to eye with him. Not because he suspected him of something, but he resented him for using his skills and not treating him with respect or paying him fairly. They often argued about that and Almanc didn't care to change. Agryn held that against him until the day when the tension between them became very high and they faced off in real fist fight. Since then, they never again saw eye to eye.

Despite Almanc's warning to Akam to stay away from Dani, Akam kept meeting with him. By now Almanc sensed that Dani was a threat, and something had to be done.

A few days after Dani and Akam met, Akam was gone and no one knew his whereabouts: not even his brother. Almanc instructed a member of his terrorist group to take care of Akam. He did not go after Dani but decided instead that Akam might slip in one of the conversations with Dani, so it was time to eliminate any chance that may happen.

Agryn was furious that he didn't know what happened to his brother and he had no information to help him find him. He thought Dani might know.

"Do you where my brother is?" He asked Dani with a disturbed voice.

"No, I haven't seen him since the last time we had café," Dani replied. "Does he usually take off like this?"

"No, never," Agryn replied. "If he contacts you, please tell me," Agryn asked in broken English.

"Sure," Dani said.

Dani's first thought went to Almanc. He had a feeling he had something to do with Akam's disappearance since Akam told Dani about Almanc's warning.

Some weeks went by and there was no news about Akam. Agryn met with Dani a few times, but there were no clues to help them find Akam.

"How well do you know Almanc?" Dani asked.

"Little," Agryn replied. "Why?"

"Do you think he knows where your brother is?" Dani asked.

"I don't know, Agryn sighed. "Do you think he knows?"

"I think he does," Dani replied.

Agryn pulled his phone out of his pocket very quickly.

"What are you doing?" Dani asked.

"I am calling him," Agryn said.

"No, wait a minute. You will raise suspicions in him that you believe he knows where your brother is," Dani proposed. "I know that Almanc has something to do with Akam being gone."

"I'll kill him!" Agryn interrupted.

"I don't think that's a good idea. Sure, you can kill him but either you'll die, or you'll go to jail, and I don't think you want either of those two," Dani said, trying to get Agryn to cooperate with him.

"I want to help you find out if Almanc is behind it, but you need to help me expose him," Dani offering to help.

"What can I do?" Agryn said.

"I know from Akam that Almanc is preparing for some major operations. I am not sure what operations those are, but I think they're operations to harm people." Dani was making up a story.

"I don't know anything about that," Agryn refused to believe that his brother had said that.

"If you are afraid that Almanc will get to you, don't worry about it, I can take care of him. We have to stop him, today he took your brother and tomorrow who know what he may do to you or to others."

"What are you saying?" Agryn asked. "Why do you want to stop him? Did he do something to you?"

"I want to get him for Akam and before he hurts others," Dani replied.

Agryn agreed to help Dani.

"You act like nothing is happening; keep working with him, but I need you to tell me who he meets and where he goes," Dani instructed.

Agryn kept working for Almanc without saying anything to him about his brother's disappearance, but he kept tabs on every move and every meeting Almanc had. He would follow him and take photos of him while meeting with other people.

A week later Agryn brought Dani the information he asked for. Dani sent a quick text to Carl with the photos of Almanc and his associates. He showed the names of the people Almanc met with who were identified as members of the Kurdish Guerillas and another cell known as the 'Iman Group Movement'. They were a group of mobsters disguised under the flag of 'better future and prosperity for all', when in fact this group was formed to conduct extorsion, murder, drug trafficking and money laundering. The main objective was to sell drugs to terrorist members to get high so when they kill, they have no remorse. They are not in control of their actions. It was all purely illegal business transactions.

Dani and Agryn met with Carl.

"This is Carl, this is Agryn," Dani said, introducing the two. "Carl and I are US secret Service agents. The US government has had the Kurdish Rebellion and the other groups in their sights for some time now. I know for a fact that Almanc killed your brother, but I couldn't tell you before. It is a matter of time before he gets you because he knows that if you confront him about your brother, he will have no choice but to get rid of you."

Agryn, barely able to keep tears from running down his face while thinking of his brother, took a big sigh before saying to Dani, "You're sure Almanc killed my brother?"

"Yes, I am."

"I know you want revenge," Carl injected, "but we can get the guy who killed your brother."

"How?" Agryn asked.

"You'll have to go to him and ask him to help you find your brother. We will wire you and we'll listen to everything he says," Dani said. "You need to be careful not to seem angry. Act normal and we'll take of the rest."

"Your job is to get him to either talk to you or introduce you to someone who can help you," Carl said.

Agryn met with Almanc, asking him to help him to find his brother. At that point Almanc, acting arrogant now that finally Agryn lowered himself to ask for help said to him,

"I don't know where your brother is, but let me ask around. Maybe someone has some information."

A couple of days later Almanc said to Agryn, "meet me at this address."

Agryn contacted Dani to let him know the latest news. The three of them; Carl, Dani, and Agryn met to wire Agryn before his meeting with Almanc.

He made his way to the address he had been given, walked into the same apartment with the computers, phones and transmitters. Four people were inside the apartment working on some equipment. One of those people was the one who took care of Akam but didn't know that. Almanc started speaking in Kurdish.

"He needs help finding his brother," he said. "Anyone have any information for him?" he demanded.

"We'll ask around," they all replied.

That was the end of the request for help. Immediately Almanc asked his men again in Kurdish if everything was ready for the operation.

"Yes, we are," one of the guys said. Another one asked "what about the people around, what do we do?"

Almanc in Kurdish, replied, "it's collateral damage; we can't think of the people around, if they are there then it's their problem. The operation must be successful, that's all I care about. We'll meet here at the time we agreed on," Almanc ordered his terrorist members.

Carl and Dani were not too far from the apartment and heard Almanc's conversation. Almanc and Agryn left the apartment and Agryn thanked him for his help. At the end of the alley they split up, going different directions, but before they split Almanc shouted from a distance at Agryn, "be here at the same time as the others."

Agryn didn't answer, he just nodded his head in agreement. He rushed to Carl and Dani, quickly taking off the wire. "I cannot stand seeing him or being around him. I should kill him," Agryn said, very upset.

"We'll get him," Dani reassured Agryn.

That same day, on a Saturday evening Carl, Dani and two more agents parked close by the apartment waiting for Almanc and his guerillas members to make their move. At 7:45 pm, they saw all of them leaving with bags. They followed them, wondering where the terrorist group was heading until Dani yelled, "

Son of a b****ch! They are heading toward the Istanbul Turkish Merkez İş Alanı or the Financial District, which also houses the US-Turkey Chamber of Commerce!"

"Don't lose them," Carl shouted to the agent who was driving.

"Why the Financial District?" the other agent questioned.

"It's the busiest place in the city, especially on the weekend," Dani explained.

"Sons of b***ches want to cause as much damage as they can," Carl said.

The pursuit was on, but Carl, Dani, and the other agents were not sure what to do. They could just wait until Almanc and his terrorist group arrived at the City to arrest them, but they might lose them in the crowd and that was too risky. Carl told one of the agents who spoke Turkish to make the call to the police. The call was anonymous. Dani dialed 155.

"Allo!" The switchboard officer replied.

"There are three suspicious guys carrying bags, and they are heading for the Financial District. You need to send some officers to check them out," the agent said.

"What's your name?" the switchboard officer asked.

"That's not important. You need to send someone; do you hear me?" the agent replied.

"It's okay," the switchboard officer said.

"What do you mean 'it's okay?'" the agent angrily asked. "If something happens, you're responsible," the agent said before ending the call.

The agent threat got the switchboard officer moving and he dispatched some officers to go check the area.

Upon arriving to the Financial District, Almanc and his members parked their car on the side of the street and Carl, Dani, and the agents parked across the street hiding behind a row of trees. They could see Almanc getting out of the car and looking around before the other two guys got out and started heading toward the Turkish Stock Exchange building. Almanc plan was to cripple the Turkish economy and at the same time cause as many causalities as possible.

Carl and his team were getting ready to get out of the car and follow when they saw two police cars pull up followed by an unmarked SUV. From the SUV surfaced four people in civilian clothes, probably undercover secret agents. They started walking, looking like they were checking the area, when one of plain clothes officers caught a quick view of one of Almanc's guys right before he turned the corner of a building. He was carrying a duffle bag on his shoulder. He gestured to his partner to go follow the guy with the bag. Once they turned the corner, they saw him walking fast like he was in a hurry to be somewhere. They stayed behind him. At one point they ordered him to stop, and he turned around, looked at them and took off running. The chase was on for about two blocks, when finally, the guy decided to dump the bag and keep running. The agent stopped to check the bag and found a wired bomb ready to be connected. But the guy did not get far before one of Carl's agents cornered him, not too far from where he dropped the bag. As soon as he came around the corner of the building, Carl's agent had him on the ground.

"Where are your friends? he asked him in Turkish.

"Which friends? I don't know what you're talking about," he replied.

The agents searched him whole holding him down and found a piece of piece of paper in his pocket of describing exactly where the bombs were to be placed. The guy had some mental condition from a fall on his head when he was young. It affected his ability to remember, so he wrote things down to remember them. The piece of paper had a drawing of the area where the bombs would be located.

The agent immediately contacted Carl, "I know where the subjects are heading."

"Where?" Carl replied.

Carl and Dani rushed to the area, making their way through the people on the street. After finding a bomb in the bag, the police were now convinced that the anonymous call that came in confirmed that the Financial District and the people were in danger, and they called in more forces. People did not understand what all the commotion was about. Some thought maybe there was a fight taking, place, other thought maybe it's a robbery, and others thought maybe someone was shooting a movie scene. The agents sealed the area after clearing the people out but Almanc and the third guy were not located yet by the Turkish police.

However, Carl and Dani knew where they were from the piece of paper retrieved from the guy they accosted earlier.

Carl and Dani snuck behind the barrier the police put in place and split up, each going in the direction of where the two remaining bombs were supposed to be.

First, Carl entered the building where Almanc's guy was, using a Turkish police jacket that he took from the hood of the police car. Almanc's guy was hiding in one of the rooms, connecting the bomb to a device to remotely detonate it. Carl was going from one floor to another but could not find him. That is when he reached for his phone and called his agent. "Does the f******g paper you found on the guy tell you which floor the bomb might be?"

"Hang on", the agent said, checking the drawing on the paper, "the 7th floor," the agent said. "S**t, that's where the Turkish international and largest bank in the country is," he murmured to himself.

He knew the location from some previous work.

Carl was still searching. He got to the 7th floor at the same time as Almanc's guy. With his gun raised, he ordered him to stop and drop the bag. The guy looked Carl and ran towards the elevator. Realizing that it would take a few minutes for it to come back, he ran towards the stairs with Carl chasing him Halfway down the staircase he dropped the bag and pulled out a knife, coming back at Carl, but Carl didn't fire. He wanted him alive. After a fight, a few cuts and punches, the guy was on the run yet again and this time, jumped, through a window from the 7th floor killing himself. Carl retrieved the bag and took it back to the police chief. The police chief didn't know who Carl was and didn't really care to know. For him so long as he had the bomb, and disaster was averted, things were good.

However, he asked Carl, "who are you?"

"I work in this building. I am with the US-Turkey Chamber of Commerce," Carl replied

"It's Saturday. Offices are closed today," the chief probed.

"We have a big meeting on Monday, and I needed to get some paperwork ready," Carl said.

"Thank you, sir, for your help." The chief said with a smile.

Carl nodded his head as a welcome gesture and left.

Dani, on the other hand had entered the second building through the delivery entrance in the back of the building. This entrance was never locked when security was there because security agents used to go out for smoke breaks. Inside Dani avoided all the cameras by waiting until the cameras turned to the opposite side before he ran to the next place. He didn't know where Almanc would be, but he knew he was there and that he used the same entrance Dani used to get in. Almanc and his gang had already scanned the area and the buildings and knew that back entrances were always unlocked. He searched in every place but couldn't find him. He decided to check one of the bathrooms. He had a feeling that Almanc wasn't too far and that perhaps he would be in one of the bathroom stalls where no one would be able to walk on him and disturb him connecting the bomb to the remote detonation device. Sure enough, Dani went in slowly opening the bathroom door and he heard some noise. He quietly walked in and saw a bag on the floor and knew right then that he had his terrorist. With all the force of his right leg, he hit the stall door, knocking Almanc against the back wall of the stall, but Almanc didn't stay down. As a trained guerilla fighter, he was quick to stand up and he charged towards Dani.

"I was sure you were not some person looking for work," Almanc said in perfect English.

He spoke several languages perfectly. It's part of the training they go through to blend in within different cultures.

"And I knew you were an assassin and nothing more, you son of a b***ch terrorist," Dani replied.

"I am going to finish you off just like I did with Akam. And his brother's next," Almanc threatened before grabbing hold of Dani.

Dani tried to free himself; he punched him but Almanc didn't flinch and he was still holding Dani.

Dani felt like he was overpowered by the 6'2" Almanc. He kept punching him while he was in his grip and then in a sudden move, Almanc threw Dani past the swinging bathroom doors into the hallway, where he had more space. Dani stood up and rushed to an office that was open. Almanc followed him and he tried to grab him again, but this time Dani was quick to grab him first. They held on to each other and both fell on a desk with Dani at the bottom. Before Almanc could put his hand on Dani's neck to strangle him, Dani glanced quickly to his side and grabbed a stapler and he shot Almanc twice in the neck. Almanc was in pain but still fighting. But he lost control for a minute; just enough time for Dani to liberate himself. He grabbed a pointy envelope opener and stabbed Almanc in the stomach, making him fall to the ground. Almanc held his stomach with one hand, bleeding, while leaning on the desk. Dani pulled him down tying both his hands with his shoelace and left him on the ground. He went back to the bathroom, grabbed the bag, came back and dragged him to the elevator. He delivered him to the police chief along with the bag.

Once again, the chief was wondering who these people were - actively catching the terrorists - but this time he did not ask Dani any questions. He realized these two guys must not be just ordinary citizens who happened to catch Almanc and his terrorists' group.

While all this was happening, the chief received a call from the police commissioner inquiring about the situation

"Two strangers captured the group," the chief said.

"What do you mean, strangers?" the commissioner asked.

"One of them said he works in the building here and the other, well, I am not sure who he is," the chief confessed.

The commissioner was quiet for a minute. He knew the Americans never left Turkey. The commissioner was already made aware by the Chief of MIT (Turkish Military intelligence) from his meeting with Carl that American spies were still operating in Turkey.

"Those were not strangers," the commissioner told the chief of police, they were American secret service agents, "you need to find them," he ordered.

But by then Carl and Dani were long gone. The police looked everywhere for them and couldn't locate them. Every hotel, the airport and other cities were inspected, but there was not a trace.

The final police report of the investigation and the arrest didn't mention anything about two Americans involvement in the apprehension of Almanc and his group. The story was told that the Turks, with the help of some informants, got the job done. After all, this was a matter of national and international pride and any information that diminished their success would otherwise jeopardize that pride.

Carl and Dani hid in the safe house for few days to cool things down before they left Turkey. They crossed the border to Bulgaria after almost 15 hours of driving. James contacted a friend of his to drive them across the border. His friend was a former US agent and had been living Turkey for 10 years after he retired from his post in Germany. James had known him for many years when they were both new recruits at the CIA. They formed a strong relationship that lasted all these years. The hunt continued for Chanaf, Fenak,

and Assad. Chanaf was arrested in his mansion while sleeping at night. Agents broke into his house and arrested him without any incident. Fenak was also arrested trying to flee the country under an unsummed name and a fake passport. He was arrested boarding a ferry to cross the Mediterranean Sea to Europe after he paid someone to help him escape. As for Assad, he was found hanged in his office. Based on the medical examiner report, it appeared that he used his own tie to kill himself.

Carl decided it was time for him to head to the US to take care of some personal business and to spend time with his family before he went on the road again. As for Dani, the only place that made him feel at home was where he spent the last few years building a new life. He went back to Spain hoping that nothing had changed since he left. He wanted to find the same welcoming city he had grown to love and spend every moment in it; he wanted to cherish the memories of his life and that of Jane. He knew that his life was never going to be the same since that first encounter with the US Secret Service and as time went by, he came to accept that his new life as 'a man with many identities'. For now, he was going back to Spain and he was happy to have a place he could call home for the time being. As for his future, he left that to James Foster and Carl Hooper.